ROTTEN RHYME

A SUSSEX STEAMPUNK TALE

BY
NILS NISSE VISSER

ROTTINGDEAN RHYME – A Sussex Steampunk Tale
Written by Nils Nisse Visser
Cover Design by Corin Spinks
Cover image of Alice: ©Heijo Van De Werf
Licenced by Dreamstime.com ID 50210580

Published by CBS GREEN MAN PUBLICATIONS
Brighton, Sussex, January 2019
ISBN: 9789082783667
NL NUR-CODE: 333

This story originally appeared as **'The Rottingdean Rhyme'** in the 2017 Writerpunk Press anthology *WHAT WE'VE UNLEARNED: ENGLISH CLASS GOES PUNK*

Copyright text @Nils Visser

Poetry (adapted):
'A Rottingdean Rhyme' is a steampunked version of Rudyard Kipling's 'A Smuggler's Song'

Poetry (original):
'The Secret of the Machines' by Rudyard Kipling
'Sussex' by Rudyard Kipling
'A Three Part Song' by Rudyard Kipling
'Sussex Wunt be Druv' by W. Victor Cook
'Green Sussex' by Alfred Tennyson

All Rights Reserved. No part of this publication may be reproduced, stored in a retrieval system, or transmitted in any form or by any means, electronic, mechanical, photocopying, recording, or otherwise, without the prior permission of both the copyright owners and the above publisher of this book.

This Sussex Steampunk Tale is dedicated to the owners, staff, and regulars at the Yellow Book steampunk pub in Brighton.

CONTENTS

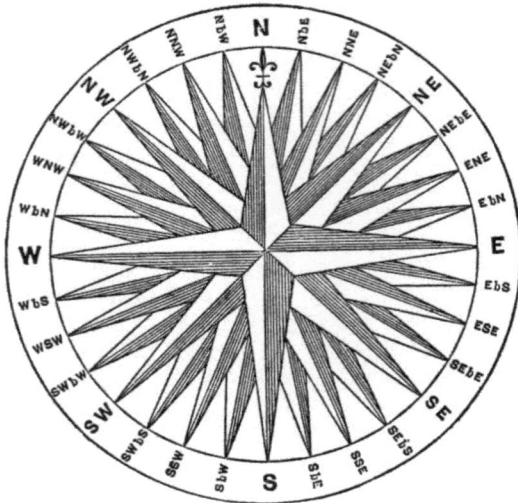

ROTTINGDEAN RHYME

BY NILS NISSE VISSER

A SUSSEX STEAMPUNK TALE
BASED ON
RUDYARD KIPLING'S POEM

A SMUGGLER'S SONG

MACKELLOW-FEATHERLIGHT
PUBLISHING
BOUNDARY PASSAGE
BRIGHTON-NÉE-HOVE
SUSSEX, ENGLAND

1869

IN CO-OPERATION WITH

WRITERPUNK PRESS

SEATTLE, VICTORIANA COLONY
BRITISH AMERICA

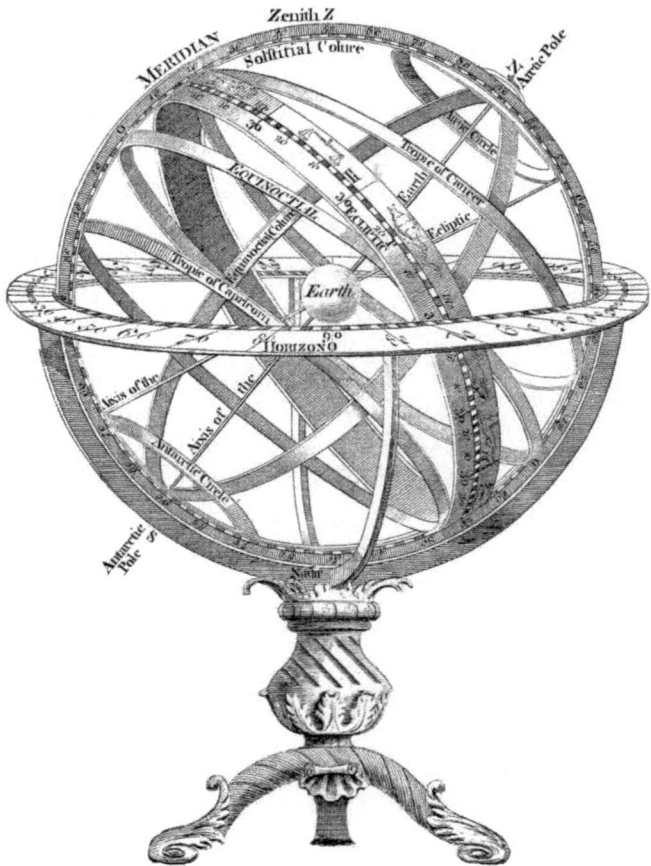

PROLOGUE

The village seems dark and silent, but not everyone is asleep. Cottage doors are opened and shut, as quiet as can be. Furtive figures make their way through the twittens and streets. They don't carry torches or lanterns to light their way. They don't greet each other. They tread softly, to minimalize the sound of their footfalls. They make towards the shingle beach.

It's busy there. Shadowy shapes move between the parked fishing boats, focusing their attention on a handful of them. As they work, these particular vessels take on a different shape. Outriggers with propellers are attached to either side of the hulls. Gas canisters are retrieved from shacks, their content transforming bulky bundles attached to the top of masts into inflated envelopes.

Although people work as quietly as they can, some noise is inevitable, but barely audible over the continuous crash of waves on the shingle beach, as well as the rattle and hiss of shingles as the water withdraws again.

The man in charge of operations paces between the small aeroships. He's done this more times than he can remember, but he's nervous. Two figures, much shorter than the rest, approach him. Are they truly ready? He thinks they are, but still, he worries. It is no small thing to send them out over the sea on this moonless night.

1. IT ALL STARTED WITH ALICE

Five and twenty skyskiffs
Skirring through the dark
Brandy for the parson
Baccy for the clerk
Laces for a lady
Letters for a spy
Crystals for a clocker
Round shot to make rozzers cry
Watch the floor, me darling
Whilst proud aeronauts skirr by
Atween the silver stars
In a black and moonless sky.

(From *'A Rottingdean Rhyme'*, by Yardrud Pilkin, 1869)

The door squeals a horrendous protest when I push it open. I stop the motion halfway and find myself in an instant quandary. No matter what I do next, there'll be more rasping from those obnoxious wrought iron hinges.

A seagull sailing over the Green shrills laughter at me, its shrieks spurring me to come to a decision. I squeeze through the gap, make a rapid turn, and shut the door in one quick movement.

The noise is worse. My heart sinks at the grating metallic squawk which I'm sure must have been heard all the way to the village's narrow shingle beach.

I turn to face the congregation gathered in the nave of St Margaret's Church. Rather than facing the chancel, all heads in the nave are turned my way, all eyes on my intrusion, all ears expectant of further disruption I might cause.

My brief self-perception of being a clownish attraction at a travelling circus dissipates when my eye catches the coffin. I've come to St Margaret's to attend a funeral. I look around the sea of faces and deliver a series of mournful nods as earnestly as I can to emphasise that I've come to pay my respects.

What does that sea of eyes in the nave behold? A young man, in his late twenties, scraggly curls of dark hair, round spectacles, somewhat nervous in his disposition, and seemingly frail for a man in his prime. His ill-fitting clerical clothing and ink-stained hands single him out further as an outsider, a *Sheere-man* as the locals call it. A *furriner* who hails from beyond the Sussex county borders. Worse than that even, a *Lunnoner* from *Lunnon*.

This is my second year in the coastal village of Rottingdean, where even a grandparent from a neighbouring county will mark one as an *outlander* of sorts. Normally speaking, my presence in the tight-knit community's midst on such a grave occasion wouldn't be appreciated. However, my uneasiness at

5

intruding is allayed when the first villagers nod in greeting, to be followed by the others, a few adding a sad smile of welcome. I have, to some extent, integrated myself into the community over the past few years, and this is a poignant moment of acceptance. I am motioned to take a seat on one of the back pews.

Once positioned there, I sneak glances at those in my vicinity. The faces around me all share a common denominator; the permanent marks of weakness and woe Blake had penned about with such eloquent harshness in his treatment of London.

The villagers lack the pale pallor which marks the poor of London, being far more exposed to the elements by life in a fishing village, but these are a lean people nonetheless. They are weaned on the minimal, taxed mercilessly, and hardest hit by even minute price rises for daily staples. These fishing folks have to be a hardy lot to survive. The children are the only ones not yet marked by the grim and gaunt determination that results when folk are chained to a life of scraping together a meagre existence from one day to the next.

The villagers' eyes turn back to the coffin. Only one face is still turned to me, that of a young girl in the front pew. She's wearing her Sunday dress, and a mourning veil through which I can see her eyes brimming with tears and lips trembling with the effort to remain composed. Nonetheless, she manages a poignantly brave smile.

I return the smile, not only in acknowledgement of her pain, but also because she was the trigger, the reason I have come to claim my place in this community today. After all, it had all started with Alice.

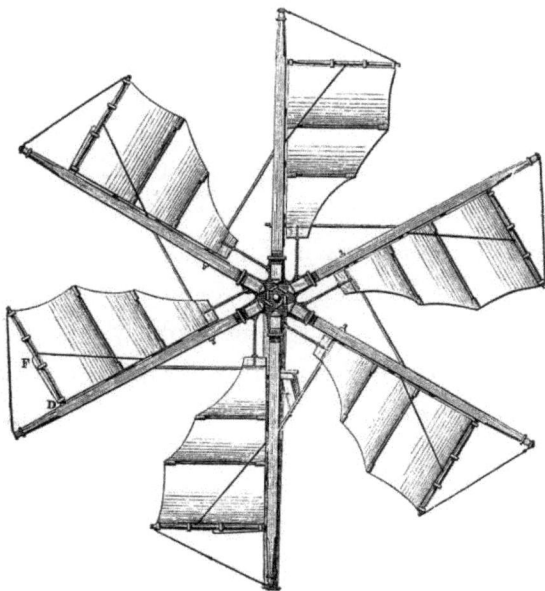

2. EGYPT IN THE BACK GARDEN

If you wake at midnight
And hear a propeller's beat,
Don't go drawing back the blind,
Or looking at the sky.
Them that asks no questions,
Isn't told a lie.
Watch the floor, me darling,
Whilst proud aeronauts skirr by.

(From *'A Rottingdean Rhyme'*, by Yardrud Pilkin, 1869)

I met John Hawkeye's daughter before I got to know the man himself. In many ways, Alice was the first person I met properly in Rottingdean. Alice and her friend Brax. During my first wintry months in the village, folk would greet me politely on the rare occasions I ventured outside my little cottage. There had always been distance though, a wariness in their eyes as they carefully appraised the stranger who had appeared in their midst, unannounced and uninvited.

I had inherited the cottage from my uncle, my mother's brother Ned Twyner, one of the village fishermen. The cottage was sparsely furnished and equipped with only basic conveniences. It sufficed for I cared not for luxuries. The sober environment fitted the mental den of misery in which I found myself a prisoner. Pining for her night and day, she who had broken my heart. I won't name her here, as she plays no part in this particular tale, other than being the cause for my sudden departure from my life in London, and my melancholy mood at the start of this story.

Somewhere in that first cold and dark winter season, the image of her sincere open face and the sound of her melodious laugh began to lose their sharp and painful focus in my memory. Truth be told, when spring arrived I half suspected that I was pining for the sake of pining, having somehow found comfort in the sense of ominous doom I had contrived to envelop my entire existence in.

I was so wrapped up in these moods that at first, I failed, or perhaps refused, to notice the advent of the new season at all. I kept my shutters closed to ward off the first tentative warm days, the budding haze of green on the branches of the hitherto barren trees and undergrowth, as well as the cheerful birdsong which started to compete with the ever-present shrill cries of the seagulls.

Thus, spring caught me by surprise when, towards the end of April, I ventured into the cottage's extended back garden; a long strip of unkempt wilderness. I had been there before, of course, daily to visit the outhouse, but always with my eyes fixed on that destination, caring little for the sprawling brambles and dead weeds which surrounded a few desolate apple trees and dilapidated sheds that served only to remind me of my own withered soul.

This time though, I walked out of my back door with a different purpose, my curiosity having been aroused by the rhythmic beat of propellers.

I was born and bred in London, where I had barely even registered skybound aeronauts, so commonplace is the passage of aerocraft over the imperial capital. On the rare occasions that I ventured out into Rottingdean however, I had noted just a few, always in the distance as they skirred their way to or from Hollingbury Aeroport on the outskirts of the nearby seaside town of Brighton.

The age of steam seemed to have bypassed Rottingdean altogether. Its small fishing fleet was oar and sail powered, the local notables made use of horse-drawn carriages to get about, and all spoke in hushed tones of the wonders which could be seen in Brighton; the gas lights and steam powered vehicles on the land, out at sea, and in the sky.

On this afternoon, hearing the distinctive beats of a propeller seemingly right over my back garden, I walked outside, thinking upon how quickly a once common noise can become so rare that it's immediately noticeable to the ear. Outside I marvelled at the sight of a low flying skyskiff, its oblong envelope darkened and single stack at the hull's stern belching smoke. One of the crew waved, but not at me. Instead the greeting seemed to be directed toward the end of my long garden, which sloped upward to meet a meadow on a hill flank.

Upon scrutiny of the wilderness at the garden's end, I was surprised to see a small figure jumping up and down with glee; a young girl, one of the village children I had seen around before a few times.

The skyskiff chugged inland, skirring low into the vale which shelters Rottingdean, the village cosily nestled between Beacon Hill, Mount Pleasant and High Hill, there where the curvaceous green Downs and ragged chalk cliffs meet on the edge of the English Channel.

Since I was outdoors already, I decided to investigate the garden, curious as to why a gleeful child was to be found at the back of it.

The journey was quite an adventure. The rigour of forcing a path through the tangle of weed and undergrowth drew me out of the melancholy stupor which had made me feel old beyond my years. I felt refreshingly invigorated when I reached the small clearing at the very end of the garden, some seventy yards from the cottage's back door.

Apart from the girl, whom I estimated to be six or seven years old, there was also a boy of her age, squatting next to a patch of freshly upturned earth in which he was rooting about with grubby hands. Part of the old stone wall which separated my garden from the meadow beyond had collapsed, explaining how the children had gained entry. There was a small stone smoking shed with a slate roof in the corner of the clearing, in front of which was a rudimentary table and benches built from various bits of scrap wood.

The girl was sitting on one of the benches, playing with a doll which seemed far too fancy for a village child to own. It portrayed a female aeronaut and had a delicate porcelain face bearing an eternally frozen smile. The doll was dressed in a fine lace blouse, miniature leather corset, skirt, and a velvet hood; all a stark contrast to the girl's own frayed dress.

"How do, *Mus* Pilkin?" The girl seemed entirely unperturbed by my presence, somewhat to my surprise because I had half-expected the children to dash out of my garden and into the meadow upon my arrival. I was also surprised that she knew my name.

"Erm, mustn't grumble," I answered. "May I ask who you are? What you are doing here in my garden?"

"Ah!" The girl placed her index finger along her nose. "Mum always says that when a stranger asks I am *naun* to tell them where no one is, nor yet where no one's been, *Mus* Pilkin."

I smiled at that, my first smile in a long time but how could I do other?

"But who is the stranger here?" I countered. "For you know my name and I know not what either of you are called."

The girl considered this, her face animated by lively thought. "I think you are correct, *Mus* Pilkin. My name is Alice and this here…" she held up her doll. "Is Ebony, all-along-of her long black hair. She's French, you know."

"I am pleased to meet you Alice. *Bonjour* Ebony. And who is this young man here?" I pointed at the boy who seemed oblivious to my presence, still rooting about the earth.

"Brax," Alice said.

The boy turned around, gingerly holding up a fat earthworm which wriggled between his fingers.

"*Iiiiiiiii, iiii, iiiih*," he said.

"I am pleased to meet you Brax," I said, before turning back to Alice. "Is Brax…special?"

"We are all special!" Alice laughed. "But Brax is *bettermost* special all-along-of him speaking Worm right now."

"Worm?"

"Worms have their own language. Brax is the only human in the whole village who can speak Worm," Alice explained.

"*Iiiiih*," Brax said, before turning back and gently lowering the worm onto the patch of soil.

"I see," I said.

"Brax is very clever, cleverer than you or me, *Mus* Pilkin," Alice declared solemnly, watching the boy with admiration in her eyes.

"When have you had the chance to measure my intelligence?" I asked, somewhat offended, for I prized my intelligence as my one redeeming feature. Alice looked confused, so I rephrased my question. "Why do you think your friend Brax is cleverer than I am?"

Alice laughed. "You are very silly *Mus* Pilkin. Why, Brax is proper Sussex, you're *Sheere-folk*, my dad says all *outlanders bain't* right in the head, all-along-of being *furriners*."

I pulled a funny face, the kind I suspect those who '*bain't*' right in the head might display, and the girl squealed with laughter.

"So now you know our names," Alice said brightly. "Which means you are the stranger again, *Mus* Pilkin, for Brax and I have been here forever and longer, and you haven't."

"Forever and longer is a long time, Alice. How old are you?"

"Seven, which is a long time, I will be eight next year! Brax is seven-and-a-half, so he will be eight sooner." She said the latter solemnly, as if the fact was a tragic circumstance of life she had wearily resigned herself to. "I've been here since forever ago, and Brax a mite longer than that."

"I concede you have been here longer than I have. But as for not telling me where no one is, or has been, I do believe that you are very much in my garden, so I know the answer to that question already, don't I?"

I looked around, taking in the old coloured glass bottles arrayed in a row by the side of the old shed, frayed ribbons hanging from the branches of an old gnarled apple tree, and groups of sticks arranged in crude geometrical patterns, stuck in the ground where the weeds had been cleared. Looking into the old shed I saw a few chipped teacups and saucers neatly lined up on a crude shelf, and a carefully swept floor. The children had made themselves a veritable secret kingdom and I envied them their imagination which undoubtedly made this Wonderland of theirs come to life.

"*Mus* Twyner said we could play here, *Mus* Pilkin," Alice said defiantly. "Wait!"

The girl disappeared into the shed. When she reappeared, she was carrying an old metal biscuit tin, holding it with the reverence due to a treasure chest.

15

The tin did indeed appear to function as such, for when Alice opened it I could see some coppers, items of broken jewellery, glass marbles, and more of such things. She took out a small envelope from which she retrieved a folded letter that she handed to me.

The paper was damp and musty, so I unfolded the note carefully, not wanting to tear the paper. I recognized the spidery handwriting of my uncle straight away. I had seen it in the letter he had written to me just before his death, informing me he intended to bequeath his cottage to me, his closest living relative after the death of my parents in a cholera epidemic during London's Great Stink back in '58.

Rottingdean, June 1867

I, Ned Twyner, being of sound mind and ailing body, do hereby grant Miss Alice Kittyhawk and Master Braxton Beesworth the right to play in the Ancient Egyptian city of Thebes (at the end of my garden) for ever and longer.

Signed: Ned Twyner

"Thebes?" I asked

"I am the Pharaoh of Thebes in Egypt." Alice nodded gravely. "Brax is my High-Priest. Sometimes my cat Bubba plays a palace lion." She pointed at the shed. "That's the Royal Palace."

"*Grrrr*," Brax growled, and then snapped his teeth a couple of times.

"Is he speaking Lion now?"

"That's silly! Brax is speaking Crocodile," Alice corrected me. "We throw trespassers to the crocodiles in the Nile you know. The Nile is a big river, much bigger than the Ouse and Cuckmere put together."

"I have heard of the Nile. I always thought Pharaohs had beards?"

"How silly *Mus* Pilkin! I am a Pharaoh without a beard, so that means Pharaohs without beards exist."

"*Cogito ergo sum*," I conceded the point.

"*Quiddy?*" Alice asked, using the broad Sussex dialect to query my Latin.

"I think; therefore, I am," I told her. "Words from a wise man, forever ago as you say."

"Puh." Alice shrugged. "I could have told you that too, *Mus* Pilkin."

"I do believe you could," I said truthfully, quite taken by the brightness of the clever little girl. She was like a breath of fresh air, reminding me how musty I had grown. I continued speaking, enjoying the game: "But I have a problem now, oh Ruler of Rulers."

"What's that *Mus* Pilkin," Alice said. "Mayhap I can help you. I do like to help people."

"Why maybe you could help me, Your Highness. You see, if I am to honour my uncle's contract with you and allow you to play in my garden, it is like ceding part of my property to another country. That would mean I am clearly trespassing in your kingdom of Thebes at the current moment."

Alice thought about this for a while, then brightened: "That means we get to feed you to the crocodiles!"

I nodded solemnly.

Brax growled and snapped again.

"Brax says to show mercy," Alice said. "How very disappointing, don't you think so *Mus* Pilkin?"

"Highly disconcerting, especially for the crocodiles. By-the-by, I thought only Brax could speak Crocodile."

Alice placed her hands on her waist and looked at me sternly. "You must listen better, *Mus* Pilkin. He is the only one who can speak Worm. I can speak a little Crocodile."

She growled and snapped her teeth. "Do you hear?"

"My humble apologies, Your Highness, I must admit I am a little silly."

18

"Yes, you are," Alice said. "But Brax likes you, so I will show you mercy. We shall call Thebes Upper Egypt, and the rest of the garden Lower Egypt. You can go into Lower Egypt any time, but to come to Upper Egypt…"

"I will need a Royal Invitation."

"Very clever! Yes, a Royal Invitation. And this time you may leave Upper Egypt without being eaten by crocodiles."

Brax growled his approval.

"Thank you, oh Ruler of Rulers." I made a bow and shuffled backwards. Alice waved at me regally until I was out of Upper Egypt and turned to make my way back to the cottage.

I felt uplifted. The brief visit to the children's secret kingdom had allowed me to see the world from a different perspective, something which might inspire new reflection upon my circumstances. Apart from that, I naturally felt relief to have escaped the terrible fate of being fed to the crocodiles, for I had little doubt that it would have been a gruesome end.

That evening, there was a knock on my front door, just after I had partaken of a simple meal of bread and cheese.

I looked around, seeing the unwashed dishes, the unswept floor, a tabletop mostly concealed by my ink pots, notebooks, and sheaves of writing paper. I felt a light panic rising at my total unpreparedness to receive a visitor, but also a great curiosity as to whom it might be, rapping so unexpectedly at my door.

Opening the door, I saw a broad and tall man, his shoulders adjacent to top of the low doorway. The man bent down his head when he perceived that the door was opening. His face came into view. It was drawn by time, wrinkles which spoke of a lifelong habit of laughter and mirth, a greying mop of hair and an unkempt silver beard.

"Begging your pardon, *Mus* Pilkin." His voice was deep and booming. "For intruding on you unannounced, *howsumdever*, I understand you had a narrow escape earlier today."

"I beg your pardon?"

"There are *dunnamany* crocodiles in the Nile, *sureleye*. My daughter told me she spared your life after you trespassed in Thebes."

"Alice!"

"Yarr, Alice." The man stretched out a great gnarled hand. "I'm Jonathan Kittyhawk, though most call me John Hawkeye."

I took his hand and shook it. "Yardrud Pilkin, most people call me Yard. I was somewhat surprised to find an extension of Egypt out back."

"I served in the Royal Navy, *somewhen*. Stationed out there for a while, shared *dunnamany* recollections with Alice."

"They must have made an impression on her then. Do come in Mr Ki…Hawkeye."

"*Bethanks*, don't mind if I does." John Hawkeye had to stoop to enter. When he raised himself again he expertly avoided one of the low beams stretched along the ceiling as if he had visited many times before. His eyes roved around, taking in my slovenly habits before resting on the papers which covered the table.

"Ned told me you were a scribbler."

"I was a clerk in London, but not anymore. There isn't a great demand for my skills in Rottingdean."

"*Mayhap* you can try in Brighton. There's something of everything and everything of something in Brighton," John Hawkeye said. He pointed at some of the papers which were covered in writing. "Yet you write?"

I was uncertain, hesitant to admit I dabbled in poetry to a man who probably earned a living by hauling fish out of the sea. It made me feel like a fraud somehow. I mumbled: "Just some words, Mr Hawkeye."

"Words are *bettermost*. I like words. Do you mind if I sit down, *Mus* Pilkin?"

"No, of course not!" I cursed myself for my poor hospitality. "Can I provide you with a beverage? A cup of tea perhaps?"

"No *bethanks*. I'd appreciate hearing some of your words though, *sureleye*." He seated himself at my table and looked at me expectantly.

I looked through my papers somewhat nervously, having never before shared my private musings with anybody. I dismissed the arrangements which were nothing more than soppy yearnings for the woman who had broken my heart, selecting instead a more recent effort which I thought might please him.

We were taken from the ore-bed and the mine,
We were melted in the furnace and the pit—
We were cast and wrought
And hammered to design,
We were cut and filed
And tooled and gauged to fit.
Some water, coal, and oil is all we ask,
And a thousandth of an inch to give us play:
And now, if you will set us to our task,
We will serve you four and twenty hours a day!

We can pull and haul and push and lift and drive,
We can print and plough
And weave and heat and light,
We can run and race
And swim and fly and dive,
We can see and hear
And count and read and write!

"It's *deedy*," John Hawkeye said. "*Naun* shrouded in fancy notions beyond a simple fisherman's savvy, I like that."

"Thank you, Mr Hawkeye." I decided to dare a joke. "Although I doubt any of us *Sheere-folk* could confound you. I am reliably informed that we're not quite right in the head."

My guest guffawed. "I'll wager my Alice told you that." He leaned forward, to look me into my eyes. "Tell me, *Mus* Pilkin, do you feel quite right in the head, at this moment?"

I was taken aback by the forwardness of the inquiry, the sheer directness of it, the astute reading of my troubled soul. Unable to answer verbally, I shook my head to indicate I didn't feel quite right in the head. I didn't add that I felt as if I had lost myself, much as I suddenly wanted to confide in this man.

"I reckoned as much," Alice's father leaned back again. "You're half a Twyner, a good family, been here *dunnamany* generations. And the Twyner in you is wont to 'preciate being in the country, instead of *Lunnon*. It *bain't* healthy, I reckon, to live in big cities. *Howsumdever*, your words now, they are fine words, middling clever. It's just that the subject don't quite agree with me. Plenty of honest hard-working folk been replaced by those infernal machines you praise, tis unaccountable. Friends of mine, good farmhands,

23

left with *naun* choice but to present themselves and their *fambly* at the gate of Brighton workhouses."

"But the advances made….!"

"'Tis a marvel, *sureleye. Howsumdever*, is it used to advance the country as a whole?"

"Just think of transportation, why to get from London to Edinburgh now only takes…"

"More money for a ticket than I could scrape together, *Mus* Pilkin. It's all very well, for them gentlemen and ladies to go frolicking about with the latest gadgets, for fine folk to skirr around the world weaving the clouds and planting the Union Jack on an island here, a city there…*howsumdever*, tis been achieved by *bannicking* over the rights of common men again and again. One bad catch is all it takes for our children to go hungry in Rottingdean, *Mus* Pilkin, one drought *enow* to sink us in lifelong debt. How civilised is a nation in which little *chavees* go to bed hungry? Tis just my middling opinion, but *sureleye* the notion of civilisation be more than just a matter of whirring cogs and gears?"

I was surprised. All my life I'd been imbued with the notion of London as the centre of a great empire, and our rapid succession of technological development as the crowning glory of a great civilisation. I'd never had cause to feel anything but patriotic pride in the logical prowess of technology, the interminable precision of mechanics, and the sheer brute power of machinery. Even though I played no personal part in it, I had often felt that I was a participant in the excitement of it all, the highly optimistic sense that there were no limits beyond the reach of human brainpower. At worst, I'd felt discomfort when I rubbed shoulders with London's vicious classes, but I hadn't ever connected their dire poverty with the technological progress mankind had made.

"I suppose there is that side to it," I admitted.

"'Tis unaccountable. *Mayhap*, you ought to try and write about Sussex one day. My favourite words are about Sussex."

To my surprise, he started to recite:

Some folks as come to Sussex,
They reckons as they know -
A durn sight better what to do
Than simple folks, like me and you,
Could possibly suppose.

But them as comes to Sussex,
They mustn't push and shove,
For Sussex will be Sussex,
And Sussex wunt be druv!

I smiled because the words certainly seem to reflect local attitudes.

"Sussex folk be as stubborn as pigs," John Hawkeye said proudly. "'Tis unfortunate, *mayhap*, as it also means it takes us a while to get used to *outlanders* such as yourself, as well as their fanciful notions and refined ways."

"I assure you, Mr Hawkeye." I laughed. "I am not at all refined."

"You wear your trade on your hands. Tis how I likes to see it. *T'also* means, I reckon, that we can get by with Yard and John, instead of all this middling mister business."

I looked at my hands, covered in ink stains. For the first time, I felt proud of the smudges. "Yes John."

"That be good, Yard. Sussex is a *bettermost* place, God's Country, our forefathers called it afore the Normans came," John expounded. "Listen to this."

I'm just in love with all these three,
The Weald an' the Marsh an' the Down countrie;
Nor I don't know which I love the most,
The Weald or the Marsh or the white chalk coast.

"That's lovely!" I exclaimed.

John appeared to be pleased with my reaction. "*Mayhap* the Spring weather will encourage you to explore some of Sussex for inspiration, Yard. Mind you, I *bain't* telling you what to do, tis *naun* of my *purvension.*"

"I appreciate the advice, John," I said. "I will endeavour to explore."

He nodded and then changed the subject: "Am I to understand you *bain't* minding the *chavees* playing in your garden? They can be a middling earful when they *yoyster* about, *tmight* interfere with your scribbling."

"They are welcome to," I said without hesitation.

"That were what Alice told me. *Howsumdever*, she can interpret words in a peculiar manner of her own *somewhen*, being the *stocky* lass she is. I thought it best to come and ask."

"She's a clever little thing."

"And very precious to me," John smiled before becoming straightforward again. "I also thought it *bettermost* to come and take a measure of the man whose garden the *chavees* would be in."

That hadn't even occurred to me, but it made sense. "I understand."

"Which I would *naun* be telling you, Yard Pilkin-Twyner, if I had reckoned you were *naun* to be trusted." He rose from his seat. "*Bethanks* for sharing the words, I'd appreciate hearing more *somewhen*. Ye be welcome in Rottingdean."

3. NOISES BELOW THE FLOOR

If you see the stable-door setting open wide
And goggled crew blackening canvas inside
If your mum mends a coat cut about and tore
And your dad cleans cutlasses and guns galore
Bettermost you see naun
And don't ask naun more.

(From '*A Rottingdean Rhyme*', by Yardrud Pilkin, 1869)

A few nights later I had cause to wake in the depth of night, after a restless sleep fraught with tossing and turning. My anguished mind, that night, was trapped in a merciless, infinite loop of reliving my disastrous courtship and humiliated retreat from my former life.

At first, I thought the noises I could hear were just a part of my haunted dream state, but the dreams started to recede while the voluble disruptions increased steadily. I opened my eyes and stared at the ceiling as I tried to ascertain what precisely the noises were. Whatever else, they contained far too much of the inexplicable. Clicks, knocks, bumps, and thuds below the floorboards.

For a surreal moment I feared that I had woken in the midst of Poe's *The Tell-Tale Heart*, hearing things none other could, my fragile mind shattered at last. Reason banished these thoughts, deducing instead that my cottage had a cellar which had somehow escaped my notice, and an animal, a fox perhaps, or else a curious young badger, had found a way in.

The noises however, far exceeded those I imagined a solitary fox might make. There was clearly more than one of...whatever was down there.

Anxiety was replaced by smouldering anger. The cottage had grown on me, I felt safe there, nurtured even. It was all I had to show after half a lacklustre career keeping the books for a London shipping company. Barring the Ancient Egyptian enclave at the back of the garden, the cottage was mine, had begun to feel like mine. Whatever was making that noise was intruding on my peace of mind which already had much to contend with. I left my bed to get my much-neglected broom and drummed on the floorboards with the broomstick.

After a dozen angry taps, I stopped to listen. All sounds had ceased but then I heard soft murmurs and the light tread of footfalls on a stone floor, both sounds fading away fast. As the peace returned I got back into bed, though for good measure I took the broom with me to keep within hand's reach, just in case I would need it again.

My imagination excels most when it attempts to frighten me with insidious scenarios. From this perspective, it was odd that I hadn't consider the possibility of a haunting until the next morning, after daylight – that far less fertile breeding ground for flights of fancy – had replaced the darkness of the night. Nonetheless, once seeded the notion took hold and started to grow in my mind until it dominated my thoughts with possible spectres of the past. Wanting the issue addressed before nightfall, I decided to seek out John Hawkeye.

I found him at The Black Horse on the High Street, enjoying a tankard of ale. The tavern dated back to medieval times and had retained enough antique ambiance to momentarily make it appear as if John was a 17th century pirate on the trail of Spanish doubloons. He greeted me warmly, invited me to sit down, and insisted on getting me a tankard of ale.

"I was wondering," I said. "If you know anything about the history of my uncle Ned's cottage."

"'Tis old," he remarked. "*Somewhen* it feels as if the whole of Rottingdean is stuck in the wrong middling century, *sureleye*, all the more so when you return after striding to Brighton and back."

I smiled. I had thought the same before, but it was curious hearing it from one born and bred here. I pursued my queries: "Has anything...odd...ever happened in the cottage? Something strange?"

"Yarr," John grinned. "*Someonetime*, involving myself, Ned and a small barrel of brandy…" He paused, threw me an inquisitive look. "Has something happened Yard? To make you ask?"

I decided to tell him everything that had occurred that night. I was half afraid that he would laugh at me and dismiss my fears. Instead he took it all in with a thoughtful look on his face. He drew a deep breath when I finished.

"I'll set your mind at ease, Yard," he said. "There *bain't shims* in Ned's cottage."

"*Shims?*"

"Ghosts. *Naun* of that." He drummed the table with his fingers for a moment, his brow furrowed in thought. "*Mayhap* you could meet me tomorrow morning, when the clock strikes nine. It'll be easier to tell you all you need to know."

"I could meet you. Where should I be at nine?"

"Do you *ken* Saltdean Gap?"

"I'm afraid not."

"Never you mind, I'll send Alice to fetch you at half eight, she'll take you to Saltdean Gap and then we'll talk of these matters some more, *sureleye*."

4. KISSING THE SEVEN SISTERS

Knocks and footsteps round the house –
Whistles after dark.
You've no call for running out
Until the house dogs bark.
Skiff engines sputter into life,
In the dark, on the sly,
Mooring lines released,
Engines chugging.
Take to the sky!

(From '*A Rottingdean Rhyme*', by Yardrud Pilkin, 1869)

Alice and Brax stood at my front door at half eight the next morning.

"Oh, Ruler of…" I began to say.

"Not now, *Mus* Pilkin," Alice said. "Thebes is out back, this is the front door. We're lookouts and runners today. Plain Sussex ones."

We started walking through the village, past a row of cottages and several Tudor farmhouses. I asked Alice what lookouts and runners did.

"Why, they look out and run, *Mus* Pilkin!" Alice answered.

"And drink cups of tea," Brax added, somewhat to my astonishment.

"You speak Human too, Brax!"

"Only *somewhen*," Alice told me. "Not all the time."

We walked out of the village, upwards through the fields on the slopes of High Hill.

"But how can….?" I started to ask.

"Them that asks no questions, isn't told a lie, *Mus* Pilkin," Alice reprimanded me. "*Bettermost* you see *naun* and don't ask *naun* more, my Mum always says. *Somewhen* things are just the way they are."

It was surreal to feel like a young pupil in the presence of a venerable master, when the latter was all of seven years old and the much older pupil obliged by convention to be at an age where some wisdom should have been mustered. I chose to salute the absurdity of it and recognize common sense when presented with it.

Brax was content to leave it be as well, busily imitating every birdcall his ears perceived, with considerable skill I might add.

"You're very good at speaking Bird, Brax," I complimented him.

He frowned at me. "I weren't speaking 'bird', *Mus* Pilkin, just whistling."

"Forgive me, I am a little bit…"

"Silly." Alice finished my sentence. "I think I am getting used to it, *Mus* Pilkin."

"That is a relief to hear, Alice. Brax, what is your favourite bird?"

"*Oeh-oeh, oeh-oeh.*"

"He likes *owling, Mus* Pilkin."

"Hooting," I corrected Alice.

"*Naun*, in the Downs country we say *owling*," Alice insisted. She giggled. "It's a joke as well. *Owling* is also the other thing folk do when they sneak out at night."

I was greatly taken aback by this last insight from a seven-year-old child and chose not to respond to it.

We reached the apex of our route across High Hill. Grateful for the distraction, I stopped to marvel at the view. Behind us the tower of St Margaret's and the rooftops of Rottingdean appeared most serene and picturesque, contrasted by the bare grassy dome of Beacon Hill which rose up behind the village. On its height stood the black-tarred Smock Mill, where the village corn was ground, a glowering black monolith which looked like a primeval giant guardian from our viewpoint on High Hill.

On the other side of High Hill, we had a view of a half-bowl of open Downsland. The higher slopes were covered in stretches of thorny furze which bore a blanket of yellow flowers. Lower down was a patchwork of fields around a few isolated farms. The bowl ended abruptly along the sea, the lower grassland within reach of salty sea-spray during spring tides, the upper slopes ending abruptly in ragged cliff edges.

"Saltdean Gap, *Mus* Pilkin," Alice said. "If you walk past Lower Bannings Farmhouse, over there, there's a second barn past the first barn, just after the copse of birches. Dad's there, but Brax and I must go back to Rottingdean from here."

"*Chip-chip-chip tell-tell-tell,*" Brax said.

"He's not whistling now. *Mus* Pilkin," Alice told me. "Now he's speaking *Caffincher.*"

As our ways parted I could hear Brax speaking *Caffincher* for a while yet, his call repeated by chaffinches in the vicinity.

"*Cherry-erry-erry, tissy-chee-wee-oo.*"

Ambling through the pleasant countryside I found my way to the second barn without ado, there to be struck by a magnificent sight.

In front of the open barn doors was a chaser, its keel resting on a wheeled wooden trailer, the aerocraft's oblong envelope fully inflated. The chaser had an extended stern tapering up towards a narrow poop deck behind the engine room. The mack rising from the engine room's low roof, clear of the back of the envelope, was smoking already, and I could hear the mechanical stirrings of the engine. The sails were all furled, wound around their yards which were tied alongside the railings of the weather deck, ready to be deployed. The outriggers bearing the propeller cases, one abeam each side of the stern, were folded out, the propeller blades ambling slowly in their circular course.

"How do, Yard," John Hawkeye boomed as he came striding out of the barn, followed by a young man who was about eighteen years old and dressed in respectable clothes, the sleeves of his coat incongruously covered in oil stains.

"Fine, thank you, John, how are you?"

"Scratching along," John answered. "This here is *Mus* Volk from Brighton. Magnus, this is Yard Pilkin, our village poet. Yard, Magnus is even more *outlandish* than you are, you'll be pleased to know, all along of him being a migrant, come striding all the way from Germany he has. Tis unaccountable."

"My parents left Germany to come here," Magnus corrected him. "I am Brighton born."

I shook hands with the young man who seemed pleasant enough, but soon mumbled something about an experiment and excused himself to fetch some large reed baskets from a nearby cart. He proceeded to transfer these to the chaser's weather deck, setting them down by two crates deposited by the raised door-house of the focsle cabin.

"Well, Yard, what do you make of *The Salty Mew*?" John asked.

"*Mew*?"

"The Sussex word for seagull."

I had never seen an aerocraft so close before. Although the *Mew* was clearly a working ship, rather than a finely styled and glossed leisure or passenger craft, there was a grace to her lines which was very pleasing to the eye.

"She's aptly named then," I said. "She's a beauty, a true mistress of the clouds, Captain Hawkeye."

"There *bain't* a finer aerocraft between Chichester and Rye and it's a *bettermost* day for skirring. You'd be welcome to come along today."

"Really?" I asked, hardly daring to believe my luck.

"By *Geemeny*, I *bain't* jesting," John answered. "Come, let's board the *Mew*."

Once on the weather deck he walked toward the helm in the small pilot house that fronted the raised door-house of the engine room. A man of my own age came clambering out of the engine room, he was short and bald, his hands stained with oil and soot.

"Fitz," John said. "This is Yard Pilkin, a regular wordsmith. Fitz is from *Lunnon* too, Yard."

"Well who'd Adam and Eve it, John?" Fitz asked John as he nodded at Yard. "You letting two Londoners aboard *The Salty Mew* at the same time. We might mutiny and skirr the *Mew* home to the world's vilest den of sinful vices."

"I protest," Magnus joined us, his baskets safely secured. "It is Brighton which has earned that title. Royally bequeathed to us by the Prince of Pleasure. We refuse to share it."

"By *pize*, Magnus, you Brighton Jug," John said. "Proud of being sleazy, tis unaccountable."

"Both Downies and Wealdfolk are proud of being as stubborn as pigs," Fitz pointed out. "Compete with one another to see who's most stubborn while them in Brighton maffick about in a festive stew. Woe us, Yard, a pair of poor honest Londoners surrounded by sleazy pigs!"

Although their words were antagonistic, their manner of banter was amiable, and I sensed the geographical rivalry was mostly in jest.

"So proud of your city, Fitz," Magnus said. "That you have hidden London from view behind a filthy curtain of fog and smoke; smeared it in soot."

"I like smearing things in soot," Fitz leered. "I'm regular Brightonesque in my tastes."

Magnus ignored him and turned to Yard. "Were you as surprised as Fitz here was, to discover that Sussex raindrops aren't coloured dirt brown with mucky grey streaks, such as they are in London?"

"Somewhat," I confessed honestly.

"Sussex also got the *bettermost* mud in the whole of England, *howsumdever*, I *bain't* planning to *scorse* pleasantries all day," John said.

"No point in gongoozling here like windy-wallets, Cap'n," Fitz agreed. "Engine is good to go."

"Let's see to the mooring lines then lads," John ordered. "We'll cast off and see if we can catch the wind."

Not much later the *Mew* was in steady ascent, her propeller casings inclined diagonally to let the beating blades provide an upward lift. John, Captain Hawkeye now, nosed the *Mew's* bow to larboard to set an easterly course.

I stood by the larboard railing near the pilot house, absolutely enthralled by the sight of the ground slowly falling away, the farm houses and a small row of cottages nearer to the sea taking on the quality of toy buildings in the playroom of a wealthy country house.

At first there seemed to be no wind at all. I could see the trees below us dancing slowly in the day's brisk breeze, but the *Mew* seemed to exist in a windless state until the Captain stopped following the wind by setting a slightly divergent course. Then, and only then, was my hair tugged by moving air.

I was employed in helping to unfurl the sails, the dorsal sails on the main yards and the pectoral sails on the fore yards. The crab-claw shaped sails billowed out as John found a shear to skirr along and we started making good speed, still ascending though we were beginning to level out.

The views were spectacular. Aft of our stern were the regimented rows of rooftops of Hove, Brighton and Kemp Town; the recently opened West Pier visible behind the Royal Suspension Chain Pier along the seaside promenades. To larboard I could see the town of Lewes in its great amphitheatre of chalk hills, as well as the prominent rise of Mount Caburn. Ahead of us the Ouse river valley wound toward the sea, bypassing the large embankments of the fortress at Newhaven, before running into the harbour sheltered behind its protective breakwater. Behind Newhaven's harbour was the town of Seaford abaft of which rose the majestic white cliff of Seaford Head.

Fitz returned to the engine room. Through the open door I could look down into a maze of pipes and machinery, red and yellow valves throughout as well as switches, levers, and uncountable gauges. Fitz moved from one gauge to another, peering at them with a grin or a frown, adjusting a valve here, fiddling with a lever there, before heaving more coal through the fire door of the boiler.

Though the engine and pumping pistons produced a considerable amount of noise it wasn't as much as I had expected.

"A remarkably quiet engine," I complimented John. "I thought you didn't approve of machinery."

"'Tis a useful tool," he answered. "A two-cylinder triple expansion aero-engine. Fitz is a *bettermost* fitter, he fine-tuned it to perfection."

"What is Magnus doing?" I pointed at the young man who was unpacking rolls of rubber coated wire and cables, as well as mechanical gadgets from his baskets by the focsle.

"He told me," John scratched his head. "*Howsumdever*, I cannot recollect the details. Tis experimental, young Volk is a heretic, a proper heathen."

"Heretic? Heathen?"

"In this age of steam, he is most insistent that another new-fangled power source is *bettermost*. Elektreksi or some such new-fangled nonsense."

"Electricity! He adheres to Michael Faraday then?" I asked.

"Yarr, elektreksi, that were what I said. I've heard him say that Faraday name *otherwhile*. Young Magnus is *deedy*, already an inventor at his age. He'll *fay* well, mark my words. Tis due to him that we're skirring today, he has an experiment on his mind and paid for the helium. Tis an expensive business, skirring is."

I watched in fascination as Magnus started to construct small steel rigs the length of his arm to which he attached thin tin blades, shaped like a windmill's sweeps. The *Mew* began to lose altitude now, almost imperceptibly sinking.

Fitz emerged from the engine room, wiping his hands on a rag. He looked to starboard, taking in the vast expanse of the blue sea. "Well can't we feel the shrimps! How are we skirring, Cap'n?"

"Well *enow*," John answered. "We'll take her around Seaford Head, then Magnus can muddle about while the rest of us kiss the Seven Sisters. I'll be needing full power then."

"Ah the soft embrace of the Seven Sisters," Fitz sighed. "Those gentle curves, their dainty lips…"

"Avast with your balderdash, Fitz, you *Lunnon scaddle*" John admonished him, "you're making young Yard blush."

Fitz pointed at the town of Seaford, which was coming into view on our larboard prow. "Better a '*Lunnon scaddle*' than a Seaford Cormorant, is what my gran always told me."

"Your gran who never left *Lunnon*?" John asked.

"The very same," Fitz answered defiantly.

"*Bettermost* you see *naun* and don't ask *naun* more," I jested, repeating the words I'd heard Alice say earlier.

John shot me an inquisitive look. "We'll make you proper Sussex yet, Yard, like a Twyner ought to be."

"What is this about the cormorants?" I asked.

"The good folk of Seaford," Fitz supplied. "Have been known to get very enthuzimuzzy about salvaging shipwrecked hulls."

"Forever ago. Brave attempts to save the lives of *dunnamany* doomed sailors," John said piously.

"Make a stuffed bird laugh!" Fitz snorted. "Ships lured in by false harbour lights, finding sharp jagged rocks beneath their keels instead of a safe berth, ain't it?"

"There may have been some of that, but *naun* Sussex ships, just *Sheere-folk*," John admitted with a sly grin on his face. "Though *somewhen* these old tales are *dubersome*, to be taken with a pinch of salt. At any rate, I reckon tis better to be a Seaford Cormorant than a Hastings Chop-Back or a Rye Mudlark, and I *dursn't* even speak of a Worthing Pork-Bolter."

"Yarr Cap'n," Fitz exaggerated a salute. "I'll shut me tater-trap and go mafficking about in the engine room."

Fitz looked at me. "Now don't you go minding every word this old man tells you, Yard. I wouldn't trust these coast folks with a single roasted chestnut, cause they ain't honest Londoners like you and me, are they now?"

"Go cut your stick Fitz, down below. Don't let me catch you on the deck again," John ordered. "On the pain of a most gruesome death, *sureleye*."

Fitz descended the steps which led into the engine room. We were clearing Seaford Head, the cliffs angling inland to reveal another broad vale. It was a second estuary, marking the Cuckmere river meandering to the sea through a wide expanse of grazing marshes. Beyond that was a long line of white cliffs, their feet assaulted by the pounding sea and their crowns bright Downsland green.

"The Seven Sisters, time to take the *Mew* down some more" John said, flicking a series of switches on his instrument panel next to the helm. "Magnus! Seven Sisters *anigh!*"

Magnus, who was attaching his steel rigs to the starboard railing, waved. "I'll be ready, thank you Captain Hawkeye."

"Do you see those cottages, Yard?" John asked me. "Coast Guard cottages, just like the row at Saltdean Gap."

"To intervene with wreckers trying to lure ships onto the cliffs?"

"That were forever ago, Yard, twere in the days of Queen Bess that folk would *nurt* a ship onto the rocks. *Lunnon* were at war again, with Ireland. Tax increases competing with rising food prices, the harvest wiped out by *coarse* weather…days, weeks, months of hunger. *Naun*, these cottages be much newer, tis them *pized* Coast Guards sealing off most of the coast, unaccountable that it be."

"Ah, to stop the smugglers." I knew that Sussex folklore was enriched by centuries of smuggling, though had never looked into the details of it. I felt slightly queasy as the deck slanted downward a little, the bowsprit indicating that we were coursing down towards the sea below.

"*Zackly*, except some folk prefer to call it Free Trading when they goes *owling*."

"*Owling*, Captain Hawkeye?"

He laid a finger along his nose. "The Free Traders hoot alike owls in the dark, to talk - heard but unheard - whilst conducting their business."

"I see," I said, placing Alice's reference to '*owling*' into context. "But I thought the smugglers..."

"Free Traders."

"The Free Traders were a dying breed, on account of the Coast Guard's new methods."

"'Tis become hard, very hard indeed, to bring goods across the water these days," John nodded sadly.

I looked along the length of the row of imposing peaks of the Seven Sisters, the almost vertical cliff faces and the sea spray as waves rolled in to dash against the boulders and rocks piled up at the cliffs' feet. Bringing in anything seemed hard enough without the Coast Guard adding their clout to the fray.

"Some folk, *howsumdever*, say that the Free Traders *bain't chuckle-heads*. That they have evolved, found new resources…" John tapped the smooth polished wood of the helm. "…new ways of crossing the coast."

"I understand," I said calmly, though my mind was all a jumble as I digested his meaning.

"These same folks," John continued, "say that *somewhen* the Free Traders might just be storing some goods in the old hiding places. Afore shifting them to *Lunnon*. Them secret places been in Rottingdean since forever ago."

"Cellars," I mused.

"Just so, Yard, just so. Cellars, tunnels, vaults. Most of the houses and pubs are connected, from the cliff caves beneath Beacon Hill to St Margaret's."

"So, everybody knows about it?!" I asked in loud surprise.

John didn't answer me; instead he gazed at the Seven Sisters as they started to fill our horizon.

"Them that asks no questions," I said softly. "Isn't told a lie."

"*Zackly*, Yard," John guffawed. "There's *naun dubersome* about that, *sureleye*."

"Did my uncle Ned….?"

John grinned. "Ned were a Free Trader himself, one of the *bettermost* batmen."

"Batmen?"

"The folk who carry a bat, or other weaponry, to protect the tubmen, them what do the unloading of tubs, crates, or bales."

"Well, I shan't tell anybody," I declared. "From what I've seen it's an austere life in the village."

"Tis so indeed. Some folk, *howsumdever*, might be willing to express an appreciation for silence, and do so in coin. A mutual understanding as it were, regarding certain night time activities which *bain't* taking place beneath the floorboards."

I considered this for a moment, and then made to speak but he interrupted me.

"Think on it a while, Yard. Tis no light undertaking. If you were to say 'no' you can walk away, you'll have my word that not a hair on that unruly mop of yours will be harmed. Give your 'yarr', *howsumdever*, and it'll be a contract of sorts. One you'd be expected to keep to."

"I don't need time to think on it," I replied, surprising myself with my audacity. "There must be a fox or two which frequent my cellar. That's all I know and all I've heard."

"*Bethanks*. It looks like our young inventor is ready."

I looked at the two steel miniature rigs hanging overboard, their tin wings already spinning. Wires and cables ran from the casings the wings were attached to, through the rigs and then onto the deck where they connected with several metal boxes with gauges and levers attached to them. A third rig, shorter than the others, rose from the largest box, topped by a glass bulb containing spidery wires within.

Magnus, who was crouched down by the metal boxes, waved.

John turned to the open engine room door and hollered. "Fitz! Ready to kiss those sisters?"

"All set for some nobby snogging, Cap'n!"

"All deckhands, safety lines!" John commanded.

I had been issued with a leather harness of sorts before we had lifted off, two crossed leather bands running across my chest like an explorer's bandoliers. Upon the Captain's order, I took the line attached to the back of the contraption and clipped it on one of the many security railings running along the deck structures of *The Salty Mew*.

I watched the Captain turn towards the bow again; his eyes alight with sheer joy and determination. "Tis inadvisable, what we are about to do, Yard. For good reason too."

"What would that reason be, Captain?"

"Mark the wind, Yard. Tis blowing us towards the Seven Sisters, once we're abeam to the cliffs the wind will try to push the *Mew* against them."

I looked at the cliffs. Whereas they had seemed serenely majestic before, they were much grimmer now that they were up close, rising menacingly over our envelope as we came out of our descent. Soft embrace indeed.

"If I make a *boffle* of it," John said, "The *Mew* will be smashed into smithereens against the chalk face. There are places where there's *naun* wind at all, others where it turns and twists wildly."

"How do you know," I asked. "What is where?"

John grinned. "I watch the seagulls, young master Pilkin. Watch the seagulls and attempt to skirr in their wake."

He grinned again when he steered the *Mew* towards the cliffs, ever closer until their jagged apexes loomed over us. The aerocraft started to groan. The hull shuddered as the wind attempted to control our course. Seagulls screamed their laughter at our clumsy imitation of their graceful flight. My heart was pounding in my chest in fearful exhilaration.

It wasn't only the flight which caused my exuberance at feeling so alive. There was also the realisation of what we had spoken about. The ease with which I had agreed to become an accomplice in what the papers still described as a grave crime. Somehow it was impossible for me to even think of John Hawkeye as a criminal. He had spoken of Free Traders and I liked the name for it conveyed a notion of intrepid outlaws attempting to put right the social injustice of poverty. My uncle Ned had been one.

A few years ago, I would have rejected defiance of the law immediately, but something in me had changed. Perhaps losing everything in life had made me far more reckless, more willing to take risks.

The *Mew* made another unexpected drop, plunging twenty feet and momentarily causing my innards to feel as if they were trying to escape upwards, whilst my brain struggled to understand if we were about to die or not.

"Whoohoo!" John ululated. He swung the *Mew* to starboard just in time to avoid driving her bowsprit into the rugged cliff face.

I grinned weakly in response to the Captain's elation, although I didn't entirely understand his joy, as I was feeling positively petrified and becoming a little nauseous. I hid this as best as I could though, taking courage from the others around me.

Fitz below in the engine room, roaring an endless stream of colourful expletives at his gauges and valves, as if he could direct the engine by sheer force of personality.

John Hawkeye lost in laughter of pure joy as he anticipated the sporadic rise and fall of the wind's play around the Seven Sisters. He worked his helm, propellers and sails in perfect unison to allow the

Mew to soar within a hair's breadth of death and destruction.

Magnus Volk, intent on his metal boxes as the tin wings on the outboard rigs spun fiercely. Something sparked between the ends of the metal filigrees within the glass bulb in front of the young inventor, sparked again and then emitted light blue tentacles dancing in erratic shifts before joining to produce a yellow glow. As it brightened in intensity, Magnus threw his arms in the air. "Eureka!"

Just as we cleared the last of the Seven Sisters, skirring into calmer sky, a shower of sparks erupted from Magnus's metal boxes before there was a blinding flash and a sharp bang, swiftly eradicating the sense of relief I felt at having survived the mad dash alongside the white cliffs.

"What in Tarnation…" Fitz came running up to the weather deck.

"Young Magnus is trying to set the *Mew* on fire again," John laughed.

"Bloody hell!" Fitz grabbed a sand-filled fire pail. "Give us a hand, Yard! Grab a pail."

We ran forwards to smother the small flames dancing about the machines with sand. Fitz muttered loudly about German machine makers coming to live in England, breathing our air, buying our helium, and trying to blow up honest Londoners. I heaved a sigh of relief when the work was done. Magnus stood nearby, his dark hair standing on end, black smudges of smoke on his face. He kept on repeating: "*Wunderbar!* It nearly worked! *Wunderbar!*"

John guffawed loudly, and I found myself laughing at the madness of it all.

When I regained my breath, I said: "All joking aside, I'm relieved it's over."

"Over?" John chuckled. "It *bain't* over *yetner*, Yard."

He pointed at the bow. I looked to see we were passing a depressed segment of the cliffs, behind which they climbed to new towering heights.

"Kissing the sisters were the easy part, lad." Fitz said gleefully. "We have to bear hug the next lot, get up close and personal."

John added: "We'll pass Birling Gap *drackly*. Then comes the real work, Yard. Beachy Head, a *draggle-tail* of a headland, as *brabagious* as they come."

"I'd better get my next experiment set up," Magnus made his way to his baskets.

"Do you reckon you can handle it, aeronaut Pilkin?" John asked with some concern in his voice.

"Yard's a Londoner, he can handle it better than a hobbadehoy can handle a popsy-wopsy, ain't that so?" Fitz predicted.

I ignored Fitz's inappropriate imagery and looked at John. Grinning weakly, I said: "Aye, aye, Captain."

5. LEARNING A NEW TRADE

Dark shadows gliding overhead,
Blocking out the stars
Evading Aero Fleet searchlights
Mounted on railway cars
High up in the air,
Muffled cries and metallic scrape
As Free Traders seek
From the Aero Fleet to escape.

(From *'A Rottingdean Rhyme'*, by Yardrud Pilkin, 1869)

We became friends that afternoon, John Hawkeye and I. Friends and accomplices.

My induction into the shadow economy of Rottingdean was slow. At first it consisted merely of my polite pretence that nothing was happening beneath my feet during certain moonless nights. I learned to recognise the muted sounds of skiffs and chasers skirring overhead in the darkness. I came to know that uncommonly frequent hoots of owls signified the approach of Aero Fleet coastal patrols, or mounted Queen's Men, the Customs & Excise officers, prowling about the Downs.

I also received my payments, discreetly in unmarked envelopes pushed beneath my front door every three months or so. I used these to build up my meagre savings, although I also allocated a small sum to transform my cottage into something homelier by purchasing a set of book shelves and books. I stocked up on biscuits as well, because about once a week I'd receive a Royal Invitation to visit Thebes, providing I paid homage in the shape of tea, biscuits, and milk for the Pharaoh, her High Priest, the doll Ebony, and the palace lion called Bubba.

It took a year before I received an invitation of a different kind, issued by John Hawkeye. I answered with a hearty 'yarr' ere he even finished asking me if I might benefit from more active participation in Rottingdean's collective swindle; denying Her Majesty's government duties on goods from Holland, Flanders, and France.

I started as a lookout, generally a task for the village children. Brax taught me how to *owl* and tasked me with exercises until I could hoot to his satisfaction. On moonless nights I would take position by the windmill on Beacon Hill, or carefully prepared and concealed lookout spots along the roads and paths leading into the vale.

On some occasions I would lead a pony carrying illicit goods along concealed paths across the Downs. Those midnight caravans could contain as many as twenty to thirty such ponies, all guided to depots in the Weald – barns, pubs and churches – from where another caravan formed by Wealdsmen would ferry the goods north to London. The inland trek had many a hairy moment and inevitably culminated in regretful scenes in Wealden pubs. The combination of our great relief at having delivered our end of the bargain and fresh payment burning holes in our pockets was not a good one, and led to many memorable riotous interactions between the local Wealdsmen and visiting Downies.

When the odd shipment came in by sea, I joined just about every able-bodied adult in Rottingdean at Saltdean Gap, or at our very own short stretch of shingle, as sailors rowed goods ashore from swift Dutch cutters or French schooners. Within no time the ships would slip away into the night, their cargoes out of sight, safely concealed beneath the streets and houses of Rottingdean.

We met the aerocraft which skirred in from across the Channel further inland, away at least from the Coast Guard having a *coke* around, as John called the continuous efforts of the law to pry on our affairs. The French and Dutch aerocraft would skirr low over Rottingdean to the higher, wilder stretches of Downs between Mount Pleasant and Castle Hill. Or else they'd traverse Saltdean Gap to dip into the western fields of the Ouse river valley, guided to solid ground between the marshy grazing lands by armed Free Trader batmen with lanterns, while tubsmen waited nearby to unload the cargo.

If the Coast Guard lookouts or the Queen's Men patrols happened to hear the whirring propellers of an inbound cargo, tense cat-and-mouse games ensued. Armed patrols making their way over the misty Downs, foreign aeronauts and local tubsmen working together to unload a cargo with all haste, strings of ponies zigzagging over the network of pathways on the Downs as the Free Traders exploited their detailed knowledge of the ground.

The larger Dutch and French aerocraft, cloudclippers, skyschooners, and the occasional zephyr, would stay well away from the coast, and we would skirr to their locations over the sea in our smaller chasers and skiffs. The cargo was then transferred at dizzying heights, while lookouts kept out a wary eye for the dreaded Aero Fleet patrols.

I crewed on *The Salty Mew* on several such occasions, ever grateful for John Hawkeye's skirring skills when we had to run from the Aero Fleet to stay out of carronade range.

Sometimes the Queen's Men or Coast Guard officers would visit Rottingdean, heavily guarded by their troopers, to make enquiries. They were always met by sullen locals who professed their collective ignorance and nothing else. I lied through my teeth as well, claiming to know nothing and even less than that. There was little they could do if none of us were caught red-handed, and to their frustration the whipping post, stocks and ducking stool by the Whipping Post House remained mostly unused.

I delighted in the confusion which could arise when three different services pursued the same cause but could rarely agree on how best to do their work.

The Coastguard were the least effective. Ironically enough it was due to their efforts that smuggling had been virtually eradicated in the '30s and '40s but they had become complacent and the low pay of those stationed in the Coastguard cottages meant they were often willing to turn a blind eye in exchange for a few bob whenever there was *owling* to be done.

The Queen's Men seemed more interested in parading about in their fancy uniforms, but their clumsy night patrols could still present an accidental danger if they got uncomfortably close to our nocturnal activities.

The Royal Aero Fleet was the most dangerous opponent, many of the RAF captains of the smaller aerocraft well versed in the tricks of the trade and hard to shake off in pursuit.

Having become acquainted with every overground aspect of the business, I turned back to bookkeeping. A greater part of my task was to traverse all the underground nooks and crannies beneath Rottingdean, moving through cellars and tunnels to take tally of the casks of French brandy,

Dutch gin, Portuguese port, packs of coffee or tea, sacks of spices, and bundles of lace. I also worked on coded orders received from London, deciding which stocks were to be despatched, and arranging for the first stage of that transfer with my counterpart at the Earl's Barrel in Nickleby, near the Wealden market town of Odesby.

John Hawkeye also found a use for my less disciplined scribbling talents. Thrice I was asked to concoct suitably horror-filled tales related to two barns and a cave used by the Free Traders. The stories were retold with relish in local pubs, rapidly attaining something akin to local lore which had been around since forever ago. It gave some insurance that curious souls would avoid the places, especially at night.

This work increased my income and in my leisure time I took to visiting Brighton to read the papers in the library on Church Street, browse the town's bookshops, or call upon Magnus Volk.

The inventor was always busy, but never too busy to abstain from expounding enthusiastically upon his latest experiments and planned inventions. His driving ambition was to replace the new steam monorail, which he considered clumsy and inefficient, with a variety of electrically powered vehicles. Much to my delight and fascination he spoke of narrow-gauge railways, a sea tram, a propeller driven cabin suspended from cables, and many more of such marvels.

I had much to reflect on as I neared my third year in Rottingdean. As had become my custom, I shared my thoughts with John Hawkeye over a pint of ale at The Black Horse.

"Yarr, you've changed," he boomed. "Though I've *yetner* heard any words you might have scribbled on Sussex."

I decided to share a new arrangement I had been working on.

No tender-hearted garden crowns,
No bosonied woods adorn
Our blunt, bow-headed, whale-backed Downs,
But gnarled and writhen thorn --
Bare slopes where chasing shadows skim,
And, through the gaps revealed,
Belt upon belt, the wooded, dim,
Blue goodness of the Weald.

"Well butter my wig!" John exclaimed. "That be more like it. Mind you, Sussex is more than just the landscape. *Mayhap* you can capture its people in a poem one day?"

"I shall try," I promised.

John chuckled. "I reckon we've turned you, Yard."

"Turned?"

He answered in rhyme.

All folks as comes to Sussex,
Must follow Sussex ways.
And when they've learned to know us well,
There's no place else they's wish to dwell.
In all their blessed days.

"I can't argue with that," I conceded. "Tis a '*bettermost*' place, '*bain't*' it?"

"That it be," John raised his pewter tankard. "To your health and fortune, *Mus* Yard Pilkin-Twyner."

"And yours, Captain Hawkeye," I answered.

6. OMINOUS TIDINGS

Running round the woodlump,
If you chance to find
Little barrels roped and tarred,
All full of brandy wine
Don't you shout to come and look,
Nor use 'em for your play
Put the brishwood back again,
And they'll be gone next day

(From *'A Rottingdean Rhyme'*, by Yardrud Pilkin, 1869)

I had been on one my Brighton jaunts. John
Hawkeye had told me come to Hollingbury Aeroport
at the end of the day, gleefully adding that he could
give me a lift home. He said he had business there,
picking up various spare parts for Rottingdean's
aerocraft, as well as gas canisters.

Rather than walking, I decided to catch the
monorail service from Old Steine to the aeroport. I
got into one of the cramped carriages that was
suspended from an overhead rail and opened the
window by my seat, for it was a warm and sunny day.
I learned the mistake of doing so when we departed,
because the small engine that pulled the three-
carriage train emitted liberal amounts of hot, filthy
smoke. Industrial snowflakes of ash permeated the
cloud. Some of this mix wafted in through the open

window. My fellow passengers protested, and I quickly shut the window.

Magnus was right, I decided, the monorail had design flaws to contend with. I had visited him that afternoon, and my mind was still dazzled by the plans he had shown me for a propeller driven electrically powered cable tram.

We passed the Royal Pavilion. Even through the monorail's soot-smudged windows, the building made for an imposing spectacle. Its onion-shaped domes and multitude of minarets were incongruous in an English setting. The palm trees planted in the gardens surrounding the complex added to the suggestion that somehow a pinch of the splendour of India had been transplanted to Brighton.

I studied my fellow passengers, who made up a quaint mix. There were tourists – their suitcases piled up in the aisle –, aeroport workers in oil stained coveralls, as well as tired clerks on their way home after a day's scribbling.

That could have been me. It was me, back in London. I don't envy them.

Looking out of the windows again, I admired the gothic revival facades of St Peter's, and nearly pressed my nose against the window as I tried to peer down in through the windows of the Yellow Book pub, where I often stopped for a pint when I visited Brighton.

Despite the stuffy air and the proximity of so many people, I was beginning to enjoy the ride. I liked being elevated high above the street level, where pedestrians went about their journeys, likely oblivious that they were being studied from above. By the time we passed the Level, I had settled comfortably into the rhythmic progression of the contraption, and my thoughts were free to roam. As it was, they turned to my visit to Magnus at the Volk Workshops.

I had once seen a book in a fancy bookshop in the West End containing drawings by Leonardo da Vinci, one invention more fabulous than the next, many of them still seemingly futuristic. Those sketches on the soft creamy paper had been warm somehow; the shading of the natural materials adding rich texture, the wooden wheels teethed with pegs stunning in their prophetic vision, the three-dimensional portrayal from different angles invoking comprehension in even the dullest layman – the stuff as mechanical dreams are made on.

The sketches and drawings Magnus kept in great numbers were a contrast to da Vinci's. Clinical approaches in which measurements far outweighed aesthetic representation in importance, machine parts mapped out in detail, each computation, calibration and quantification worked out to infinite perfection.

I still liked to think da Vinci's mind must have worked like that of Magnus though; jumping from abstraction to insight and back again in an instant, capable at any moment of intense focus for days on end, during which all but the project at hand was shut out. In those moments, I supposed, a perfect fusion of mechanical theory and applied mechanics was achieved, allowing for the birth of another remarkable brain-child.

For some reason Magnus liked my company, and I was so in awe of him that I relished our friendship. We were mismatched, perhaps, but no more than John Hawkeye and I were. I felt comfortable in their company, they were real. Neither of them had any pretensions and both were, in their own way, living their life to the full, following routes they were charting out themselves, caring little as to what society might make of it.

I had seen the fine gentlemen and ladies in Brighton this day, their hats adorned with symbols of the latest fashion rage; finely crafted gears and cogs, miniature clockworks, ribbons, and feathers. Many of them had been clutching the latest edition of the French *Magasin d'Éducation et de Récréation* under their arm, containing Verne's serial *Twenty Thousand Leagues Under the Sea,* a tale which was causing furore on both sides of the Channel. I had learned from the papers that people spoke of a Cultural Revolution, though some critical voices warned of dangers involved when public adoration turned into collective fervour.

We were on the cusp of the actual worship of engineering, these critics claimed, as if science were God.

I paid it little further attention at the time, my own take being that pinning on a few silver or gold gears did not a revolution make. The real revolution, in my eyes, took place in the laboratory of an earnest hard-working inventor. Magnus, whose father had died when the young man was eighteen, leaving Magnus's slender shoulders bearing the duty of providing for his family. Or else on the deck of a working aerocraft, like John Hawkeye's *Salty Mew*, or Fitz's *Kestrel*, a winddrakar he had purchased with his profits and now skirred from the Kentish coast to Bruges and Ghent in Flanders. Roughly hewn, often foul-mouthed men who tested their craft to the very limits of what was deemed possible, equipping them with the latest improvements – often ones they themselves had devised to always stay that one step ahead of the Law.

My mind's eye supplied me with Alice's face as I clearly heard her voice, words she had spoken long ago. "*Somewhen* things are just the way they are."

I smiled because of the aptness of this wisdom at a moment of over-thinking.

We passed Fiveways, where rows of whitewashed terraced houses with bow windows stretched in all directions, as Ditchling Road climbed ever closer to Hollingbury. The monorail started disgorging most of the fatigued office workers here.

I had managed to purchase a children's book this afternoon. It featured a talking octopus called Otto, which I was sure Alice and Brax would like. Royal Invitations to Thebes had, of late, been accompanied by imperious decrees to read stories, scenes of which would later be acted out by the children in their magic kingdom. Otto would have to compete with another recent purchase though, Carroll's *Alice's Adventures in Wonderland* with illustrations by Tenniel. It had quickly become their favourite book, with both Alice and Brax asking, commanding, begging, whistling, mewling, and barking for repeat readings.

The sea of rooftops stopped, to be replaced by a wooded dale to our right, and the fields around the Withdean Estate to our left. The monorail huffed and puffed up the last steep incline of Ditchling Road, towards the industrious hive of the aeroport.

A huge rotunda had been built on the ramparts of the Iron Age hillfort which crowned Hollingbury's summit. The building's architecture mimicked the Royal Pavilion, with a large central dome encircled by smaller ones, and minarets rising everywhere. This formed the main transit hall of Hollingbury Aeroport and was also the second-to-last halt of the monorail.

All the tourists disembarked, leaving just me and the mechanical workers on board.

The view of the Downs and Brighton was spectacular, enhanced by the sight of aerocraft of all shapes and sizes skirring in on the breeze, or ascending on the wind.

A plethora of small vehicles drove to and from the transit hall: Horse drawn carriages, steam-powered trams, and – to my delight – a veritable army of electric rickshaws from the Volk Workshops. Magnus was doing very well, as John Hawkeye had predicted the first time I had skirred on the *Salty Mew*.

All these vehicles ferried crew, passengers, luggage, and light Aero Mail cargo from the imposing rotunda to the surrounding landing fields, or the various boarding masts. The latter were wrought-iron latticed towers that serviced dirigible flights making only a brief stop between London and various destinations in France and Spain. These aerocraft were moored to the top tiers of the towers, with cabin crew ushering disembarking passengers to the lifts, or welcoming embarking passengers aboard.

The landing fields were home to large luxury aerocraft, small or medium sized city-hoppers, or great long-range passenger aeroships preparing for flights to Cairo, Cape Town, Bombay, Calcutta,

Rangoon, Singapore, Hong Kong, Sydney, or transatlantic voyages to British America.

Much as I had come to agree with John Hawkeye's views that technological advances served only a few and excluded the many, I could not help but be impressed. Most of the destinations were well beyond my means, unless I fancied a city-hopper flight to London, or Portsmouth perhaps. Still, the exotic destinations instilled me with a sense of endless possibility and eternal horizons.

The monorail chugged on to the far side of the aeroport, its last stop before it looped back on the return course to Old Steine. This part of the aeroport was out of sight of Brighton, and far less pleasing to the eye. It was here that the cargo aerocraft landed between workshops, storage halls, fuel depots, and shunting rail freight engines.

I disembarked and made my way to the very edge of the maze of buildings and landing fields, where the hill dropped steeply into Coldean valley. The buildings and aerocraft were smaller here, more dishevelled in appearance. Folk here were rougher and tougher, wary of strangers to judge by the suspicious looks I received.

I was hailed by a familiar voice. It was Alice, waving from the stern of one of our new skyskiffs, *The Liddle Mew*. Soon after, John Hawkeye boomed a hearty greeting, when he emerged from a shack, carrying a crate to the skyskiff.

I responded to their greetings, and approached, admiring the small aeroship. Nothing about its appearance suggested that it was brand-new. In fact, it looked like it was on its last legs, eking out a barely sustainable existence. Rather than the sleek hull characteristic for skyskiffs, *The Liddle Mew's* hull didn't look flight-worthy, shaped at it was like the stout and rotund hog-boats used by Sussex fishermen.

All of this was deceptive, intentionally designed in that manner by John Hawkeye and Fitz Noakes. Although it was true that the bulky hull was less aerodynamic than the traditional sleek design, that was compensated by a state-of-the-art engine and improved propeller design. The 'flying hoggies' had retractable propeller riggers, and the envelope could be stowed out of sight in deflated state. It could land on water and sail just like a hog-boat. More importantly, if parked in a row of hog-boats on Rottingdean's beach, none but a wizened fisherman or local Free Trader would be any wiser.

John Hawkeye delighted in parking the new skyskiffs on the shingles in broad daylight, in full view of passing patrols of Queen's Men, there to keep an eye out on possible smuggling activities.

"Right under their noses, and the *chuckle-heads bain't* got the faintest!" He often guffawed.

"Just in time," he said, when I clambered aboard the *Liddle Mew* as he was stowing away the crate. "This be the last of it, I was hoping to leave *drackly*."

"Hullo, Uncle Yard," Alice said morosely.

"Hullo Alice, I didn't know you'd be here!"

"She's a mite upset," John Hawkeye explained. "I reckoned a flight to Hollingbury would take her mind off things."

"Am not," Alice declared haughtily.

"You were threatening to behead your dolls, oh sweet one. Tis unaccountable, *sureleye*."

"Behead?!" I asked.

"Off with their heads!" Alice exclaimed with a fierce scowl on her face.

"Oh dear," I said, feeling some guilt because I had been the one to introduce Alice to the Queen of Hearts, who was surely the one who had instilled an appreciation of decapitation in my young friend's imaginative mind. "What has caused this?"

"Nothing," Alice said stubbornly. "I'm fine."

I started helping John Hawkeye prepare for take-off, having acquired enough basic skills to help crew small aeroships over the last few years.

"Tis her friend, Brax," John Hawkeye told me.

"Off with his head!" Alice blurted out.

"What has Brax done?" I asked.

70

"Not the young lad so much, as his father and the school master," John clarified. "They took him to Brighton today, to see about a bursary. They reckon the lad is gifted and should receive further schooling next year."

"Off with their heads," Alice muttered unhappily.

"Well, you're very clever too," I told her. "Maybe…"

"Don't be silly, Uncle Yard," she admonished me. "The school master said that girls shouldn't be educated overmuch, all-along-of it confusing them."

I raised an eyebrow and glanced at John, who shrugged unhappily. "They don't half talk a load of nonsense at schools."

"So, girls can't be clever," Alice continued. Her words were at odds with the defiant look she gave me.

"For what it's worth," I replied. "I think they can be clever. Just as clever as boys, and sometimes even more so."

"By Geemeny!" John exclaimed. "That's what I been trying to tell her all day."

"Puh! You are both just saying that to make me feel better." Alice shook her head dismissively.

John gave me a helpless look, and then shrugged again. "Do you mind shifting some coal, Yard?"

I agreed readily, although it wasn't my favourite task, especially not on an aerocraft as small as a skyskiff. The engine room was cramped as it was, and soon grew unbearably hot as the flames ate into the coals that I fed into the firebox.

It was a relief to climb the short stairs which led back to the weather-deck and tell John that the engine was good to go.

He nodded his thanks, and soon after we were skybound. The wind was contrary, so the sails remained folded around the yards, and we skirred powered by steam alone.

John kept the *Liddle Mew* skirring low at first, dipping into the vale of Coldean until we were clear of the busy traffic skirring to and from the aeroport. After that we ascended, rising over Falmer Hill.

By now I had skirred the sky often enough, but I was still captivated by the experience. I gazed spellbound at the scenery. The Downs rose and fell in every direction, the lush greenery of their grassy summits dotted with sheep. The tranquil vales between them sported the darker green of trees and occasional rooftops of hamlets and farms. To the north, I could see the heights of Ditchling Beacon and the ramparts by Devil's Dyke, beyond which the patched greenery of the fields and forests of the Weald stretched for miles. To the west I could just make out the copse of trees crowning Chanctonbury

Ring, to the east the imposing rise of Mount Caburn guarding Lewes and Glynde. To the south, beyond Mount Pleasant, Red Hill, and Whitehawk, sea and sky blended on the far horizon.

The sight I remember best from that flight, however, was that of John and Alice. John had finally succeeded in taking Alice's mind away from intended beheadings by instructing her to take the helm of the *Liddle Mew*. He stood at a small distance from her, far enough to grant her independent command, close enough to intervene should that prove necessary.

Alice was listening intently to her father's every instruction as he explained the instrumentation of the pilot house to her. By the time we were skirring between Mount Pleasant and Red Hill, heading for the vale of Ovingdean, John was guiding her through gentle manoeuvres by manipulating the propeller stance.

The girl's face displayed utmost concentration and her eyes shone with fierce joy.

"I'm skirring an aeroship!" She shouted joyously.

"Yarr, Cap'n, that you are," John confirmed. "I tell you what, Alice me darling, we'll take the *Liddle Mew* out again tomorrow, out to sea, find a friendly wind shear, and I'll teach you how to skirr the sky using the sails."

"Yes!" Alice was delighted. "I want to use the sails."

John winked at me, and I beamed because their mutual elation was infectious.

Rather than parking the *Liddle Mew* amongst the hog-boats on Rottingdean beach, John directed Alice to skirr to the barn at Saltdean Gap, where he took the controls again to land the skyskiff.

"*Bain't* no reason to deflate the envelope if we're taking her out again on the morrow," he explained.

"Can I run home?" Alice asked when we touched ground. "I want to tell mum I skirred a skyskiff. And Bubba! And Ebony! Maybe even Brax."

"Off you go," John agreed.

Alice made off as fast as her legs could carry her.

John and I began to secure the *Liddle Mew* for the night.

"My darling wife is apt to skin me alive," John grumbled. "When she hears I let the *chavee* skirr the *Liddle Mew*. Howsumdever…"

"It was a sight to behold." I declared. "Took her mind off beheading half the village, and restored some self-worth…"

"I've half a mind to keelhaul that schoolmaster."

"I'll help you."

John laughed. "Can you lend us a hand getting the netting out of the barn? *Naun* reason to let any prying eyes having a *coke* about know we've got an aerocraft parked hereabouts."

We got the netting out of the barn and began the laborious progress of heaving nets over the *Liddle Mew's* envelope. After that we cut some branches from nearby trees and stuck these in the nets, to break up the form as much as possible. The result looked ludicrously inadequate from the ground, but I knew that it shielded the skyskiff from skybound eyes well enough, unless they skirred overhead real low.

"*Bettermost*," John decided, when we stepped back to admire our handiwork. "And it'll pay well, Yard, to take extra care from now on, what with Meadows and all."

"Meadows?"

"Ah. I been meaning to tell you. But it weren't a topic to broach with Alice about. Tis the Queen's Men, they have a new commander."

I recalled some small talk in The Black Horse. "Yes, of course. Colonel Morgan Meadows, wasn't it?"

"Yarr," John said, then let out a deep sigh. "A different kettle of fish from old Commander Lonsdale altogether. Lonsdale were content to muddle on until his retirement. This new one, he's young and ambitious. Second son of a Sussex squire, keen to make a reputation, angling for a knighthood and seat in Parliament *naun* doubt."

"Do you reckon he's dangerous?"

"I *ken* he's that. He made name to the east, making life harsh for the Mudlarks."

"The Marsh folk?" I was astonished. Of all the Sussex Free Traders, the Owlers of Rye and the Romney Marshes were reputed to be the most cunning and secretive. The Marshes were a world apart from the rest of the county, and a law unto themselves.

"Yarr, the Marsh folk, *sureleye*. They reckon there's never been a more ruthless and determined Rozzer."

"Ill tidings, then."

"Yay and nay." John shrugged. "*Somewhen* there be a change of guard, a new device, a new tactic, a *Lunnon* government wanting to end Free Trading forever and longer. We been playing this game for centuries, Yard. *Nowhen* has there been a time we *bain't* found ways around it. Sussex wunt be druv."

I smiled, then repeated: "Sussex wunt be druv."

He laughed. "Yarr, and that be the way tis always been, *sureleye*. And will always be I reckon. *Howsumdever*, for the time being *twill* be *bettermost* to be on our guard. Come, let's course home."

We started walking towards Lower Bannings Farmhouse, and John changed the topic to one we both took as seriously, but was more light-hearted nonetheless.

"Have you any new scribbles to share?" He enquired.

"I composed a short one during the flight home," I admitted.

John raised an eyebrow. "Have you now? I saw *naun* paper or pens."

I tapped my temple. "Up here, I'll write it down as soon as I get back."

"Well, let's be hearing it then."

I took a deep breath, then recited.

> *You came, and looked and loved the view*
> *Long-known and loved by me,*
> *Green Sussex fading into blue*
> *With one gray glimpse of sea.*

"*Zackly!* That be grand, Yard, *sureleye.* 'Long known and loved by me' indeed. *Howsumdever…*"

"I know, I know," I said hastily. "I have started one, a long one, about the people."

I didn't add that it was based on him, Alice, and all the folks I had come to know in Rottingdean.

"Be it harder to write?" John asked.

"Yes, it's easier to capture a landscape than the spirit of a people."

"I can imagine, but, by *Geemeny*, Yard, if anyone can do it, *twill* be you I have *naun* doubt. They'll be *bettermost* words, and I for one, can hardly wait to hear them."

7. ROZZERS AND REDCOATS

If you meet the Aero Fleet men,
Dressed in blue and red
You be careful what you say,
And mindful of what is said
If they call you 'pretty maid'
And chuck you 'neath the chin
Don't you tell where no one is,
Nor yet where no one's been.

(From '*A Rottingdean Rhyme*', by Yardrud Pilkin, 1869)

When the end came it caught us off guard, as it usually does, I suppose. Even forewarned, an element of surprise seems to accompany sudden – and unwanted – changes.

I had been to Brighton again, and was on my way back, on foot this time and eager to be home. It had all become so usual, that I paid little attention to my surroundings, lost in thought as I was.

I'm not sure what woke me out of my reveries. Perhaps it was just plain instinct that caused me to cease my mental meandering at once, to look up and around warily, slowly moving my head about to try and catch a sound, even sniffing the air.

I could discern the dark looming shape of the Beacon Hill windmill ahead of me, so was close to home, but there was a sound I couldn't place. One that didn't belong to an evening stroll over the Downs. A light chiming, as if a hundred little bells were tinkling. I was struck by a sudden fear, recalling the stories the locals liked to tell about the faery folk, whom they called Farisees or Pooks, most of them nasty creatures out to cause mischief or harm. I had dismissed these tales with the scepticism of someone born and raised in a city, astonished that the locals, even John Hawkeye, were steadfast in their insistence that the little people existed and were best avoided.

I frowned and hunted the sound with my ears until I could roughly place the location of their origin, almost parallel to me, on a lower path traversing the inland slope of Beacon Hill.

The chiming was joined by the nervous neigh of a horse, picked up by some of its fellows who whinnied in return.

I dropped down into the tall grass at once, my eyes wide and breathing quickened. There were no shouts or shots, so I rose on all fours to peer down the slope. The moon was just a sliver when the clouds shifted but added just enough light for me to identify a long column of uniformed men. There were mounted Queen's Men who formed a vanguard behind Coast Guard officers leading horse-drawn wagons. They were preceded by Aero Fleet marines flanking yet more wagons and carriages, and at the very front of the column was a whole battalion of Redcoats.

There was a veritable army marching on Rottingdean and I knew John Hawkeye was out on a run with *The Salty Mew* and the skyskiff *The Chameleon,* fetching lace from a French zephyr out at sea.

More noises reached my ears now, the creaking of wagons, occasional hushed murmurs of men, the soft drumming of hoof beats on the moist ground. The chiming I had heard first was caused by the horse harnesses and men's equipment, metal tinkling against metal.

A Redcoat officer summoned four of his men and pointed at the windmill. I slowly lowered myself as the four started walking up to the windmill, some fifty yards away from me. I needed to warn the village somehow but hoped to lie low until these four returned to the column. A stab of icy fear made me change my plans when I realised there were likely to be lookouts by the windmill, children even.

I suppressed a mumbled curse and got to my feet. I remained crouched down as I made my way to the windmill, just out of sight of the soldiers whose tall shakos I could see bobbing up and down over the grass. An owl started hooting on the other side of the mill, it was joined by another, the hoots urgently repeated until the call was picked up from the lower slopes of Beacon Hill, where it met the hedges and gardens of Rottingdean. Soon the batmen would emerge from their dwellings, weapons in hand, to find out what was happening. They weren't expecting the foe in such numbers though, a chilling thought.

I ran around the mill on its sea side, towards the hooting, startling Alice and Brax who were crouched down in the grass some ten yards in front of the mill. The children were staring intently at the four Redcoats who were just coming around the inland side of the mill with their muskets at the ready.

Brax hooted again.

"Uncle Yard!" Alice whispered. "What are…"

"Hush!" I hissed. "Down! Get down the hill. Stay low."

We started slithering backwards. The children were far more adept than I was and made more speed, but I didn't mind being between them and the soldiers.

There was a stiff southern breeze, fortunately so for it caused the tall grasses on Beacon Hill to sway in the wind, swelling and surging like the tide's waves conquering a beach. Any movement we might have caused in the grass would have been concealed in the wider undulations, and though the soldiers walked around the mill to peer down the slopes of Beacon Hill there were no cries of alarm. I thought I recognized their weapons as Brown Bess muskets, which suited me far better than the rifles many regiments were replacing muskets with.

One of the Redcoats tried the windmill's door. Discovering that it was locked, he called the others and they started bashing at the door with their musket stocks. Seeing an opportunity, I rose to my feet, turned, and hastened down the hill, crouching as low as I could whilst on the move. Alice and Brax copied my movement. All three of us rushed down the hill, heading for the cover offered by the village gardens.

I kept throwing brief glances over my shoulder, relieved to see the soldiers still occupied with the sturdy lock on the windmill's door, hardly daring to believe that we had made our escape when the soldiers had been so close.

One of the soldiers began to turn around.

"Down!" I ordered.

Alice and Brax, bless them, dropped at once without hesitation. Once again concealed by the long grass, I turned to peer up the hill. The solitary Redcoat was walking towards us, too far to see us, but his body language made it clear he suspected something out of place.

"Corp!" I could hear him shout. "Corp, can you come here?"

The other soldiers abandoned the door, ambling towards him, calling out jests.

"Alice. Brax." I turned to the children. "Slide down again, keep low. Hoot twice when you reach the hedge to let me know you're there, then make for the old water pump by the Green. If I'm not there in ten minutes, get home as quick as you can."

They nodded solemnly. Alice added: "You will come, won't you Uncle Yard."

"I could hardly refuse a Royal Invitation, could I, Oh Ruler of Rulers?"

"I'd have to feed you to the crocodiles if you did," Alice whispered with a grin, after which she beckoned Brax to follow her to the hedge.

I looked towards the mill, saw the silhouettes of the soldiers, spreading out in a line now. They were more than a hundred yards away, their muskets inaccurate at that distance. My plan was a desperate one, but I needed to somehow sound the alarm before that small army overran Rottingdean altogether.

An owl hooted behind me, once, twice. The children were safe. I slowly counted down a minute to give them time to start making their way to the Green, my heart pounding the rhythm of my countdown.

The soldiers began to lose interest, the tension leaving their bodies as they shouldered their muskets, began to turn...I had run out of time.

"HEY!" I jumped to my feet and started waving my arms in the air. "You bloody Rozzers!

The Redcoats shouted at each other, and then at me.

"HEY! YOU ROTTEN ROZZERS. HEY!" I shouted and then reached down for a stick I had spotted, a hawthorn branch the length of a rifle.

I picked it up and placed one end on my shoulder, aiming the other end at the soldiers.

The Redcoats called out in alarm and raised their muskets.

"BANG!" I shouted, wanting to laugh hysterically. "BANG! BANG!"

The muzzles of the muskets erupted in flame. Loud blasts rang out in the night. I dropped, half expecting to be struck by a musket ball, dumbstruck that I made it to the ground intact. Having delivered my warning, I turned and stumbled down the slope.

The bell of St Margaret's began to ring, its peals urgent in the night. My ploy had succeeded but my sense of victory at this was short-lived for I could see the column of Redcoats which had been marching down the path toward Rottingdean break into a trot.

I hurried through a gap in the nearest hedge and made my way towards the Green, which was beginning to fill with anxious villagers.

"Rozzers and Redcoats!" I shouted as I crossed the Green. "Rozzers and Redcoats! Hundreds of them!"

"Back into yer houses," another voice shouted. "Batmen to the outer perimeter!"

There were shouts and screams of alarm, fresh gunshots there where the Beacon Hill path led into Rottingdean. People started running to and fro. I ignored all of it, making my way to the old pump where I grabbed Alice and Brax by the hand to lead them to my cottage.

My mind was racing. My primary reaction was to lead the children to the maze of tunnels beneath the village, but if the soldiers discovered the tunnels Alice and Brax would be judged accomplices and sentenced to forced labour or deportation. Taking them to their own homes risked their possible arrest too, if their families were singled out, as the Kittyhawk's were likely to be at any rate.

We rushed through my low front door and I slammed it shut, grateful for a moment of respite. I harboured no illusions though, that I too might receive a visit, once again condemning the children to a dubious legal status.

"Are you alright, Alice?" I asked.

The girl nodded. "Yes, Uncle Yard."

"Brax?"

"*Iiiih*," Brax said. "*Grrrr.*"

"This isn't the time to be spea…" I stopped. "Brax you're a genius!"

"I told you so, Uncle Yard," Alice said.

I rushed around the cottage, collecting every blanket I could find, as well as my woollen greatcoat. To this pile I added a small basket which I filled with foodstuffs hastily gathered together; a stone bottle of water, some apples, a chunk of cheese, half a tin of biscuits. I also grabbed my spyglass and a pistol.

"Let's go to Thebes," I said, picking up all the stuff and herding the children to the back door.

As we made our way through Lower Egypt we could hear commotion on the Green, harsh voices barking commands, panicked screams, and every dog in Rottingdean barking with wild fury.

We reached the strip of wilderness which marked the border between Lower and Upper Egypt.

"Meow!"

"Bubba!" Alice bent low to collect her cat, a black and white tom which was jittery amidst the night's confusion.

I took the children to the small shed, the royal palace of Thebes. It was too small to store contraband and well hidden as it was, so likely to escape the soldiers' notice. I placed the basket with food in a corner and spread the blankets about in a nest.

"You two are to stay here, do you savvy?" I asked. "Wrap yourself deep into the blankets. If there's shouting or shooting, stay inside."

Alice looked at me with large eyes, still clutching Bubba. "Are you *gwoan* to get me dad?"

I hesitated.

"He's skybound tonight, *bain't* he, Uncle Yard?"

I nodded.

"Meow." Bubba struggled out of Alice's arms and strolled over to the basket to peer at the contents.

"Meow," Brax said. "Meow."

"Brax says Dad would want me to be brave," Alice said softly.

"He will be very proud already," I told her. "You have both been very brave tonight, as brave as…" I glanced at Bubba. "…royal palace lions."

"We'll guard the palace," Alice said, determination in her eyes. "Like lions."

"Yarr, like lions." I smiled at her. "Fair winds, Alice."

"Fair winds, Uncle Yard."

I left them there, in the safest place I could think of in Rottingdean on this evil night, half hoping that whatever spells the High-Priest of Thebes had cast on Upper Egypt would help to add a layer of protection.

Stepping out of the shed I could hear soldiers on the street at the other side of the row of cottages, deep rumbling as wagon wheels rolled past over the cobblestones in the direction of the High Street and beach.

I made for the gap in the garden wall and sneaked into the meadow, going halfway-up the slope of High Hill to gain a better vantage point. I was glad that I had brought my spyglass, for it allowed me to bring everything into closer view. The Aero Fleet marines and Coast Guard had stopped their wagons and carriages along various points on High Street and were now mounting large devices on the carriages. Three companies of Redcoats and the Queen's Men were lined up on the Green, the rest spreading out to the village perimeter or patrolling the streets.

Shots began to ring out from the hill slopes around Rottingdean, batmen who had made their way out with their guns and who were now targeting the Redcoats on Rottingdean's edges. The soldiers returned fire in larger numbers though their aim was wild. Other batmen had lit two bonfires on Mount Pleasant, as a warning to the returning aerocraft.

I looked towards the sea just as the first arc lights were switched on, close to the beach. The large carriage mounted lamps were swivelled around by their crew, to project their wavering beams toward the sea. The beams were by no means as powerful as the fixed lights in lighthouses and their range was limited, but this night they sufficed as they soon found their targets.

I watched in horror as *The Salty Mew* and *The Chameleon* were illuminated, skirring straight for the beach at low altitude. They must have seen the bonfires, but I could see Coast Guard cutters and Aero Fleet brigs in pursuit, cutting off any possible escape route. The regular procedures in such a case was for the Free Traders to skirr low over Rottingdean and make their way up the vale to their alternative landing places concealed on the upper reaches of the Downs.

That would take them straight over High Street.

I took a deep breath as I wondered what weapons had been mounted on the other carriages there, fearing the worst.

"NOOO!" I shouted in vain when I saw the narrow barrels of two anti-aero guns rise to greet the Free Traders as they crossed the beach.

The guns opened fire, pumping shells into the air, their bangs followed by much louder explosions as the shells disintegrated around the Free Trader aerocraft. *The Salty Mew* shuddered under the impact of shrapnel, but John Hawkeye kept his craft on course. *The Chameleon* was less fortunate. Its forward rigging was severed so that the hull swung downwards, spilling crew and bundles of lace, the both plummeting to the ground. The hull's weight pulled the envelope, now only connected by the aft rigging, toward the ground. The floundering envelope slowed the hull's fall somewhat, but nonetheless the skyskiff splintered upon impact with the High Street's cobblestones.

The Salty Mew skirred on ahead doggedly, as stubborn as a Sussex pig. I could see crew members running to and fro on the deck, John inseparable from the helm. I saw the propeller casings by the stern change to a diagonal angle and realised that John wanted to make a rapid ascent. It was too late though, two Gatling guns opened up, deadly rat-tat-tat-tats signalling that they were rapid firing hundreds of bullets at the *Mew*. I could follow the lines of the bullets ploughing through the *Mew's* hull and envelope.

John had once told me that a moderately torn envelope could keep a hull afloat for a considerable time, but the violence which the Gatlings unleashed was so devastating that the *Mew's* envelope was literally torn to shreds even as the hull shuddered under the impact of yet more bullets. The *Mew* began to lose altitude rapidly, plunging towards the Green.

Fire had broken out in the focsle, so the *Mew* was trailing flames and smoke. The pectoral and dorsal sails were as shredded as the rapidly deflating envelope was and the engine started to falter. The aerocraft began to tilt to starboard, shaking with convulsions as it ploughed into the Green where its keel splintered on impact, leaving the *Mew* to partially break apart as it slid to a halt.

I trained my spyglass on the Green. Soldiers surrounded the shipwrecked pile of debris, Redcoats on the far side, the Queen's Men between the wreckage and my own position. Two of the *Mew's* crew stumbled off the larboard side of the remnants of the weather deck to escape the now fast spreading fire.

To my horror, a Redcoat officer shouted something, and I saw a line of soldiers raise their muskets. They disappeared in a cloud of smoke when their muskets thundered off their shots. The two crew members were hit repeatedly. Both performed short grotesque dances before collapsing lifeless on the ground. Men I knew.

I could see John approach the other – closer – side of the fragmented weather deck, wielding a cutlass in each hand. I fancied what went through his mind. If he was taken alive, he would be subjected to rigorous interrogation, his wife and daughter arrested as leverage. They would be split up and sent to workhouse and orphanage. If he died tonight, Alice and her mother would at least be spared this fate. If he didn't die tonight, he would be dangling from the gallows all too soon, regardless if he confessed or not. Knowing John, he would prefer to leave this earth on his own terms, not at Her Majesty's pleasure.

I bit my lip, willing him to live a while longer but knowing fully well he would refuse to surrender.

I focused on John's face and was not surprised to see no fear there, instead he seemed to be laughing. Even though I was too far away to hear it, my memory supplied the familiar sound of his characteristic guffaw.

The Queen's Men approached the remnants of the blazing *Mew* carefully, muskets at the ready. At their flank was an officer, on horseback, his coat adorned with gold braids and piping, his hat royally plumed.

John jumped over the splintered starboard railing and saluted the Queen's Men, cutlasses held high and roaring so loud that this time I did hear his voice. "Sussex wunt be druv!"

Eerily lit up by the flames, wreathed in smoke, joy on his face, he seemed every inch the Saxon warrior hero, arisen from ancient slumber to smite the foe.

John Hawkeye tried to do just that, whooping a war cry he charged the Queen's men, ready to hack and hew a way through them with his cutlasses.

It was not to be. A shot rang out, followed by more. John shuddered and then stumbled, falling onto his knees. He struggled up, uttered one last war whoop and made to go forward again, only to be thrown back by a volley of a dozen musket balls. I saw his body trembling upon the impacts, saw him fall to his knees again. This time he stayed there, bleeding from half-a-dozen wounds, swaying, defiance still on his face.

The officer drove his horse forward. Aimed a pistol at John's head. Fired.

John Hawkeye's bulk crashed to the ground, never to rise again.

8. BETTERMOST WORDS

If you do as you've been told,
Likely there's a chance
You'll be given a dainty doll,
All the way from France
With a corset of dressed leather,
And a velvet hood
A present from the aeronauts,
All along o' being good.

(From '*A Rottingdean Rhyme*', by Yardrud Pilkin, 1869)

"Yardrud Pilkin."

A voice, seemingly from a long time away. When my name is repeated I realise it's in the here and now and I return to the present, leaving the 'then' to find recess within my soul.

It is the vicar who is calling my name. Still half-lost in pained memories, I stand up and walk towards John's coffin in the tower house between nave and chancel. I am unconcerned by the congregation this time. Instead I focus on that coffin, on my friendship with the man who lies within. It has been a long time since I walked anywhere with such confidence, back straight and head held high. John Hawkeye, I am sure, would have wanted it that way.

All I really have to offer are words. 'Mere' words some might say. Ink symbols on a pale canvas, arranged this way and that, nothing more.

John had liked words though, and the sole certainty I have in life, the only thing to really cling on to, is my steadfast certainty that words can have power concealed in them, provided they are arranged to full effect.

I stop by Alice's side, at the front pew. Brax is seated next to her, his face reminiscent of an inconsolable puppy. He even whimpers like one when I give him a small smile. I pat his head. Then Alice's. She looks up at me with big eyes and whispers: "*Bethanks*, Uncle Yard."

I walk on, to her father's coffin. Lay my hand on the simple oak wood in a last greeting. After a moment thus, I turn to face the congregation and take a deep breath, before I begin to speak.

"I have arranged the following words in a poem which I would like to dedicate to Miss Alice Kittyhawk, in honour of her father, Captain John Hawkeye."

I pause, for my voice begins to tremble and I fight to control my emotions before I continue.

"John had often suggested I write this particular poem…not about landscapes, but about people, real people, the people of Sussex. I had the honour to hear Captain Hawkeye's last words. They were: 'Sussex wunt be druv'."

There is a collective growl from the congregation, boots tapping the flagstones, knuckles rapping the pews. When the noise fades away, I resume speaking.

"And those words were much on my mind, when I wrote this poem. It's called: *A Rottingdean Rhyme.*"

Approving murmurs are the last fuel my courage requires, and I start to recite the first of the many couplets which make up the new poem, hoping that somewhere, somehow, John Hawkeye will hear my words and consider them *bettermost.*

> *Five and twenty sky-skiffs*
> *Skirring through the dark*
> *Brandy for the parson*
> *Baccy for the clerk*
> *Laces for a lady*
> *Letters for a spy*
> *Crystals for a clocker*
> *Round shot to make rozzers cry*
> *Watch the floor, me darling*
> *Whilst proud aeronauts skirr by*
> *Atween the silver stars*
> *In a black and moonless sky.*

EPILOGUE

Rottingdean's small fleet of flying hoggies is nearly ready for a midnight departure. Each skyskiff has a different destination, a different rendezvous over the sea, a different crop to collect from waiting French and Dutch suppliers.

Yard Pilkin is no longer a shy young man. Three years after Captain Hawkeye's death, he now leads the Rottingdean Free Traders with a steady hand and clarity of mind. However, when the two small figures come to a halt in front of him, by the bow of *The Liddle Mew*, he is beset by some doubt. They are so young still and Free Trading can be a dangerous business.

"Liss, Lot." He acknowledges them using their code names, as is customary amongst Sussex folk when they go owling.

"Poet," Alice replies, using his own code name, her voice steady and confident.

She's old enough, Yard tells himself. As is her Brightonian friend Lottie. Extended youth is a luxury for the wealthy, not something that can be afforded by the poor. Free Trading was dangerous, but so was working in a coal mine, textile mill, or in one of the many brothels specialised in catering for the wealthy 'gentlemen' with a taste for young flesh. Besides, Alice Kittyhawk, alias Liss Hawkeye, has become one of the finest aeronauts in Rottingdean. Even at her tender age, there are few who can outskirr her, Free Trading is in her blood and she had begged to go. Moreover, the third member of her crew is an old skydog, who can be relied upon to keep a close eye on things. Still...

"Al...Liss," Yard says. "Are you sure? There is no shame in..."

She lays a hand on his arm and smiles. "Stop fretting. I can do this."

"We can do this," Lottie adds proudly.

Yard nods. "By your command, oh Pharaoh of Thebes."

"You're still silly at times!" Alice laughs. For a brief, sweet moment, she resembles the little girl at play in Yard's garden. Then her expression changes into one of confident determination, so alike her late father's, and she scrambles aboard *The Liddle Mew*, followed by her crew.

"Fair winds, Cap'n." Yard takes a dozen steps backward, to be clear of the skyskiff as it begins to lift off. He's still worried, but mostly overcome by fierce pride as he watches Alice take to the sky.

THE END

AUTHOR'S NOTES

The original poem *A Smuggler's Song*, by Rudyard Kipling, forms the basis of the poem *A Rottingdean Rhyme*. I did not change anything in the extracts of Kipling's poems *The Secret of the Machines, Sussex* and *A Three Part Song*. The poem *Sussex Wunt be Druv* was written by W. Victor Cook. *Green Sussex* by Alfred Tennyson. Most poems are predated by the story, but such trivial details must not hinder a narrative, as far as I know poetic time travel has never hurt anybody.

Words in italics hail from the Broad Sussex dialect which was spoken far and wide in 19th century Sussex. Their contextual meaning should be clear.

I am much indebted to Writerpunk Press, which encouraged me to try my hand at this genre. My first submission, 'The Oval Sky Room', was published in 2016 in the Writerpunk Press anthology *Merely this and Nothing More: Edgar Allan Poe Goes Punk*. My contribution is centred around Lottie Carnell, who appears briefly at the very end of this novelette.

My second submission, for the 2017 anthology *What We've Unlearned: English Class Goes Punk,* was the original version of this story, entitled 'The Rottingdean Rhyme'. The version you are holding in your hands right now has seen considerable revision.

My third submission, for the 2019 Writerpunk Press anthology *Taught by Time: Myth goes Punk*, is entitled

'The Skirring Dutchman'. Alice appears, albeit only as a brief glimpse.

A further anthology submission, to an Our Write Side anthology, awaits approval and is entitled 'Jewels from the Deep'. It features 'Liss & Lot' aboard *The Liddle Mew*. Fingers crossed.

Alice Kittyhawk features as the protagonist in *Time Flight Chronicles Book 1: Amster Damned*. The next instalment will be entitled: *Brightonesque*. Further adventures are planned, a two-book series entitled *For the Love of a Republic*, consisting of Part 1: *Sussex Rising!* and Part 2: *The Rock A Nore Murders*.

A short story set in my alternative Victorian Sussex, 'Limbs', was runner up in the 2018 Steampunk Readers and Writers writing competition, and can be read on my website: www.nilsnissevisser.co.uk

Like all Indie authors, I relish reviews. These don't have to be long and complicated, a single sentence can already make a helpful difference. Apart from my website and Pinterest pages, I also have a Facebook page (Nils Nisse Visser).

Many thanks to Corin Spinks and Heijo Van De Werf for the cover artwork.

Fair Winds

Nils Nisse Visser
Brighton, January 2019

Time Flight Chronicles Book One

AMSTER DAMNED

Nils Nisse Visser

A seemingly routine missing person case brings Alice Kittyhawk to Amsterdam where she discovers that locating a missing botanist will involve delving into the murky and illicit world of temporal displacement. Working with the mysterious Ministry of Lost & Found, Alice will have to take on some formidable foes and race against the clock in defiance of the odds which seem to be stacked against her.

(Image by Jack Savage - Photographer & Digital Artist)

Milton Keynes UK
Ingram Content Group UK Ltd.
UKHW010742210923
429104UK00001B/5

9 789082 783667